Arizona Sundown

William Baer

Southwell Press

Arizona Sundown / by William Baer

ISBN: 978-1-956199-17-8

Library of Congress Control Number: 2025907979

Cover Image: *Cowboy on a Horse at Sunset*, Ginettigino (Adobe Images)

Cover Design: WB & Vanessa Jaramillo

Southwell Press, Wayne, New Jersey

southwellpress.com

For my family and friends
especially Billy

*The wilderness and the solitary place shall be glad for them;
and the desert shall rejoice, and blossom as the rose.*

– Isaiah, 35:1

I.

1884

Chapter 1

Gayleyville, Arizona

Thursday, August 28th

I heard his spurs.

I didn't see him, but I heard his spurs.

Mexican spurs.

The kind that jingle a bit, the kind with the little metal clinkers attached near the rowels. I glanced over to my left, but the sound was approaching from off in the darkness near the far end of the raised wooden street boards in front of the Dead Eagle Saloon.

I thought nothing of it.

It was dark, windy, and dusty, and he was probably just some thirsty drover who, like me, was heading toward the saloon.

I went inside.

It was a slowish Thursday night at the Dead Eagle. Maybe fifty patrons. No music. Lots of light talk. Very relaxed.

The Reichers were playing cards at one of the gaming tables in the far corner, each sitting with his back against the wall. I nodded in their direction, then looked away. To be honest, they both gave me the creeps. Yeah, I was their one-and-only deputy, but like everyone else in town I was afraid of them. They'd killed men in Bisbee and Yuma and Gila Bend and who knows where else, apparently with very little compunction. If any. Like a number of other small-town sheriffs in the territory, they were hired not because of their rectitude, but because everyone feared them, and no one dared to cross them. Say what you want about the Reichers, we'd had no crime in Gayleyville ever since they'd arrived from Casa Grande.

Yes, they might be stone cold killers, but I have to admit, they treated me fairly. I did all the stuff that they would never condescend to doing, which was pretty much everything, but I didn't mind. No one ever crossed them, and for that reason, no one ever crossed me.

I leaned my Winchester against the bar and ordered a red-eye and drained it. Then I turned around and leaned back against the bar.

Much earlier, I'd gone out to the Dragoon foothills and shot a rabid wolf that had been killing one of the farmers' livestock. It was an ugly creature, and I'm glad that I tracked it as fast as I did. About three hours. Then I headed back into town under the sunset. I remember that it was one of those big red sundowns we often get out here in the Sonora, and I rode beneath it back to town.

The kid stepped into the Dead Eagle.

I don't know what else to call him, except for "the kid." His black bandana was still up on his face, but he seemed youngish somehow. Maybe twenty at most. Except for his spurs there was nothing notable about his appearance. He was lean and trim and wore black everything. Everywhere. Black shirt, black denim pants, black Stetson, black boots. He didn't even have silver conches on his hat band. He wore his holster on his right side, with what looked like a black-butt Peacemaker. He also had a classic five-shot Walker Colt tucked under his belt in the front. You don't see those guns anymore, and this one had an ivory handle.

It was the only thing besides his silver spurs that wasn't black.

At first, no one seemed to notice him but me, as he stood alone near the doorway and looked around. Eventually his eyes settled on the Reicher brothers, and I knew the kid was trouble, so I picked up my Winchester and waited.

As I said, the Reichers were the scariest men in town. They were also the biggest. Over six feet. Over two hundred pounds. They were brothers, some say they were twins, even though they didn't look exactly alike. They were probably mid-thirties, with wavy dark hair, Texas ties, silver sheriff badges, and black/brown eyes. Eyes like a snake. They were, as I've said, well-known shooters throughout the territory, and they liked to brag that they'd once hung around with Hickok in Abilene, Texas, so they wore their guns just like Hickok did. Two Navy Colts. Two Navy Colts each. The 1851 Model, 36-caliber, with ivory handles. Handsome guns. Showy, of course, but still handsome. They always wore them like Wild Bill, in a waist sash with the handles facing outward.

Intimidating to say the least.

It took a few moments before they saw the kid and realized he was trouble. Garrick put down his cards. He always seemed a bit older than his brother, and he usually did the talking for both of them. Garrison, who seemed no less dangerous, seemed fine with mostly listening and watching. As a matter of fact, I'd never seen them argue about anything. I'd never even seen them disagree about anything. Which made them even more scary.

As the other men at the table quietly withdrew into the periphery, out of the line of fire, the brothers stared back at the kid who was still staring at them.

Intently.

The kid spoke.

"Which one murdered Cody Clayton?"

Unperturbed, Garrick smiled a bit, but his brother shook his head as if it was beneath his notice.

Nevertheless, Garrick condescended to answer the question.

"We both did."

All was silence in the Dead Eagle until the kid finally responded.

"Stand up."

Since it was clear what was coming, I readied my rifle as the brothers stood up. They seemed a cold combination of amused and irritated.

Garrick looked hard at the kid.

"I prefer to see the face of the man I'm about to kill."

The kid still hadn't lowered his bandana.

He still didn't.

Garrick tried again.

"There's no dust blowing in the Dead Eagle, kid."

The kid gave no response.

Frustrated, Garrick shook his head.

"What *are* you, kid?"

"Retribution."

Which seemed an odd thing to say, or at least an odd way to put it.

We all waited for whatever was about to happen.

Both Reichers went for their Colts.

There was a very loud crack. Sharp. Like a pop. I'm not exactly sure how to describe it. All I know is that I felt a very sharp pain in my right shoulder as I looked over at the Reichers.

Garrick took a .45-caliber in the center of his forehead, and he slammed back dead in a loud tumble against the back wooden wall.

Then crashed to the floor.

Garrison did exactly the same.

Exactly.

Simultaneously.

I don't know if the Reichers were really twins, but they certainly died twin deaths.

I looked back at the kid who was looking at me. I lowered my Winchester, dropped it to the floor, and hoped he wouldn't kill me. He didn't. Later I realized that the loud crack was three rapid discharges from his Colt .45. I also realized that he hadn't missed me. That he simply intended to disarm me.

Which he did.

Then he looked around the Dead Eagle.

No one moved.

Satisfied, he slowly glided his Colt back into his holster then walked out the saloon door into the desert darkness.

I never knew who he was, until today, but he certainly changed my life that night. I left the law and found a better and safer life. For some reason that kid allowed me to live that night in Gayleyville, which I've never fully understood until now.

WILLIAM BAER

[Clifford Pierce]

Editor's Note

I would like to be perfectly clear that the previous account and all those that follow are accurate, having been verified as much as verification is possible.

Chapter 2

Santa Maria Chapel

Friday, August 29th

I was praying.

I didn't know what else to do.

My child was dying, sick with some kind of fever, so I came to the little chapel to pray for help. It was late at night, and the small stone Spanish chapel was empty and dimly-lit with two red votive lamps. Behind the simple stone altar, there was a wooden crucifix on the wall, carved in the Portuguese fashion. Very realistic. Very tragic, very sad. With all the horrors of the Passion.

I heard his spurs.

He came in behind me, but I didn't pay any attention. He sat off to my left, near the painting of Francis Xavier. I was closer to the other side of the small chapel and its painting of Mary of the Sorrows.

We sat in the silence.

I was wondering if my child would die tonight. He was very warm in my arms.

Hot.

Then he sighed out loud.

I looked over at the young gunman, dressed in black. He looked quite handsome in the devotional lights. Wearing a gun.

"What are you praying for?" he asked.

"My child is sick," I explained.

He thought it over.

"Bring him to Rising Sun and ask for Running Brook."

"I'm Pima."

Everyone knew that Rising Sun valley was Tohono O'odham, which the white people call Papago. The Pima and Papago have often been allies in the past, especially against the Apache, but I wasn't sure if a little Pima woman would be welcome at Rising Sun.

"It makes no difference," he assured me. "He'll help you. He's even healed Apaches."

"Then I'll go," I said, gratefully.

"Can you get there?"

The Rising Sun ranch was about ten miles from the chapel.

"Yes."

I knew that I could borrow a cart and a mule.

Then we sat in the silence again.

Until I asked him the same thing that he'd asked me.

"What are you praying for?"

"Forgiveness."

[White Dove]

Chapter 3

Midnight

Saturday, August 30th

I saw him coming through the gap in the Saucedas.

Then he headed down into the valley.

He was nothing but a black speck in the far distance, but I knew it was him. I was standing inside the Rising Sun corral with a young unbroken stallion. He'd been bred by Jack, of course. He was an all-black quarter, with distinctive white pasterns above the hooves, with a mustang's temperament. Strong, wicked fast, independent, and beautiful.

He'd already tossed me twice that afternoon, so I decided to wait a bit. I wanted Jack to see me. I was only fifteen years old at the time, but I had strange new feelings. Attractions. I wanted Jack to notice me, even though I was a filthy dust-covered tomboy in buckskin pants, leather gloves, and a boy's dark shirt. But I was pretty, and I knew it. All the older women told me so. With my wide black and large Papago eyes, with my thick black mess of cropped hair.

Yes, I knew that Jack would be leaving soon, and it hurt me in my heart. In ways that I didn't fully understand.

So I watched him as he rode Night past the main house, the adobes, the bunkhouse, the gardens, the barns, and the stables. Right up to the corral.

When he was close, I hopped on my reluctant colt again and gave him a real hard ride. I was good at this. Even though I was only fifteen, I'd convinced Red Star to let me break some of the younger colts. I'm not sure if Jack liked the idea, but he finally agreed.

The colt was bucking like loco, but I could tell that I was wearing him down. He jumped and fussed all about the corral, and I refused to let him throw me again. Jack was watching, and I was determined to ride this colt to the bitter end. Which I did. Finally, the young horse had had enough, and he broke. I guided him over to the outer fence and slid over to the top rail facing Jack.

I wanted to shout, "What do you think of that, John Shannon!" but I didn't, I just sat there and waited for him to say something. Jack was never one to waste words, and I wondered how long I'd have to wait.

"How's your bottom?" he kidded.

"Perfectly sound," I assured him.

He laughed, then looked down at the black colt.

"He's a beauty."

"Yes, he is."

"As good as Night?" he kidded again.

Night was Jack's horse, his favorite stallion, which he'd bred himself. He was black just like the young colt, but with a white star between his eyes.

I shrugged, but I certainly had hopes that the young colt would end up like Night.

"What should we call him?" Jack asked.

"I've been calling him Midnight."

He liked it.

He looked at me directly.

"He's yours."

I was stunned.

Maybe I shouldn't have been. Sure, Jack and Red Star were known to be very generous, but I couldn't believe that Jack Shannon was giving me the best young colt on the Rising Sun Ranch. I was so stunned that I got stupid and didn't respond.

Jack looked up into the mountains.

"Where's Red Star?"

"The South Ridge."

"Is he angry?"

"Yes."

[Moonlight]

Chapter 4

South Ridge

Saturday, August 30th

"M^{ore?"}

By which he meant, "Do you really need any more of those things?"

He'd come up behind me.

I knew he was there, of course.

I was sitting on South Ridge high above the valley. I was preparing flints and dogwood shafts for new arrows, something that I often did when I was frustrated.

I didn't bother to respond.

He tried again.

"No one's better with a Winchester."

I looked up at him and told him what he already knew.

"Traditional weapons for traditional enemies."

He knew.

He sat down beside me and addressed the real problem.

"It had to be done."

"Yes, but not alone."

We'd grown up together, we'd inherited the valley together, and we generally did everything together. Then he went off on his own and went after the Reicher brothers, who'd killed Cody Clayton, who was our cattle-driver and our friend.

My friend as well as Jack's.

I looked at him directly and pointed out the obvious.

"It was wrong of you to go alone. You could have been killed."

I was angry, but I wasn't crazy angry. That's not the way I am. I'm more of a slow burn, and I wanted Jack to feel it himself.

He did.

"You're right. If there's ever a need again, we'll do it together."

"There'll definitely be such a need. Eventually."

He knew it was true.

"I know."

He nodded.

Fine.

It was over.

He picked up one of my finished arrows and stupidly put the tip of his index finger against the flint tip. I saw the spot of blood, and Jack, amused by his own foolishness, held out his finger. I just shook my head and smiled.

"White men," I said, as if exasperated.

He laughed.

But there was something else unpleasant in our lives, so I told him how I felt about it.

"It's hard to watch you go, Jack. For all of us."

He thought it over.

"Sometimes I wonder if I should."

"It's what your father wanted. You have no choice."

He knew it was true.

Then he put down the arrow with the rest of them.

"Maybe," he kidded, "I should keep away from these things."

I picked up my Winchester and my arrows, and we stood up together and looked down over Rising Sun.

"I'll send you everything you need," I assured him. "I'll have Jim do it."

"I know."

The ranch lay far below us near an unexpected patch of green within the wide expanse of the arid desert.

Jack spoke one more time before we mounted and left.

"I'll miss this place."

Yes.

Of course, he would.

[John Red Star]

Chapter 5

Rutgers, New Jersey

Wednesday, September 17th

We were sitting in the third row in the Latin Room in Old Queen's, the oldest building at Rutgers College, which sat up on the same hill where Alexander Hamilton's pounding artillery had covered Washington's retreat across the Raritan in 1776.

Enough of that.

I was sitting next to my new roommate, a young western rancher named Jack Shannon. I liked him. Quite a bit. He was different, that's for sure, but I still liked him. On campus, he wore three-piece suits like the rest of us, but the rest of the time, he wore black denims and black cotton shirts and high black leather boots. Apparently, there were a lot of snakes where he came from. He was mostly quiet, reserved, a bit reticent, but friendly. He knew he was out of place in New Brunswick, New Jersey, but it didn't seem to bother him at all. His demeanor was always the same.

Calm, stoic, and pleasant.

With habitual alertness.

He also had a gun, which was not allowed on campus, so he kept it in his room in our lodgings on George Street.

He also had an amazing black stallion quartered at a nearby stable. He'd railroaded the horse over 2,000 miles from some place called Albuquerque, and he checked on it every day. Sure, some of the other students rode horses or more commonly used buggies, but no one had a creature like that.

No one had even seen a creature like that.

Anyway, we got along just fine.

Surprisingly, he'd been well-tutored out west, excelling in Latin, math, and the law. He was a demon with Virgil and the Gallic Campaigns, but he mostly preferred, no surprise, Seneca and Cicero. He also liked Shakespeare, an enthusiasm he'd apparently inherited from his father.

That afternoon, Professor Austin had invited a special guest to address his students. Owen Huxley, the US Congressman from central Jersey. He was about sixty or so, corpulent, and ever-confident. I knew his record pretty well, of course, and he was the usual mix of good and bad. He was a bit too much of a believer in federal power for my taste, and, like most of his ilk, he liked to hear himself talk.

"Don't be foolish enough," he advised us, "to think that a congressman's duties end with upholding the interests of his own state in the capital city. It's imperative for us, as the civil conflict clearly illustrated, to have a federal point of view in spite of our local partisanships."

His captive audience, about thirty students, listened respectfully, mostly with disinterest, as he continued huffing along.

"We must always keep ourselves informed of the affairs of all the other states, as well as our nation's relationship with its outlying territories, and with all of the other nations of the world."

When his opening bloviations were finished, he paused. There was a polite yet faint applause. I felt sorry for old Professor Austin, slight, thin, and balding, whom we all liked quite a bit, who'd obviously thought it would be useful to have a lawmaker come to campus and speak about the law and politics. Now he didn't seem so sure, but he pressed forward anyway.

"The congressman has kindly offered to field your questions. Please don't hesitate. It's a rare opportunity."

One of the seniors whom I didn't know that well raised his hand and was recognized.

"I understand that you and the other congressmen have once again voted to raise your salaries."

It was good-natured, and Huxley smiled.

"Yes, that's always high on our priorities."

Now the fun was over, and the professor looked for another question. Then I realized that Shannon was standing up from his seat.

Huxley addressed him directly.

"Yes, young man?"

"What about the Hunter Proposition for Arizona statehood?"

It seemed like an odd question to Huxley, and he was cautious.

"Are you from New York state, young man?"

"No."

Relieved, the congressman now felt free to express his well-rehearsed opinion.

"Have no concern, son. Congress will *never* include that uncivilized backwater into our thriving nation of progressive states. It's a Hades of murdering drifters, gamblers, horse thieves, and godless marauding savages, without the slightest measure of legality, justice, or lawfulness."

I'd heard it all before, of course, especially after the reports a few years ago about the Earp shootings near a corral in Tombstone, which seemed like a rather lethal name for a town, but I still felt that "Hades" was a bit over the top even for the likes of Huxley. Everyone in the room went silent. Eerily. We all knew where Jack was from, and we wondered what he'd do. Instead, he just stood there, cool as could be, and allowed Huxley to dig himself even deeper into his hole.

"I would speculate," the congressman speculated, "that if the entire world was searched over, there could not be found so degraded a set of villains as form that territory's principal society."

It was a fine piece of demagoguery, and it led to yet another uncomfortable silence.

Finally Jack responded.

"Have you ever, sir, been to Arizona?"

"I have not."

"Then what's the source of your opinions?"

Huxley did the best he could.

"A congressmen had many sources."

"Enlighten me."

Frustrated, Huxley turned to Professor Austin for help.

"Who is this young man?"

Jack responded first.

"An Arizonan."

Then Jack stepped out to the center aisle and looked coldly at the apprehensive congressman.

"It's well-known that you oppose the Hunter Proposition for strictly political reasons involving the Hudson River Allocation."

I must admit, even I was stunned by Jack's audacity.

But he wasn't done yet.

"It's one thing to be a blowhard, a political hack, and to sell your vote to the highest bidder, but it's quite another thing to blaspheme the decent God-fearing people of Arizona."

He looked hard at the frightened congressman.

"I wouldn't do it again if I were you."

Jack turned and left the room, as I kept thinking about that gun in his bedroom.

[Erick Ramsey]

Chapter 6

Halloween

Friday, October 31st

I was sitting in my little buggy dressed like Cleopatra.

I was wearing an ankle-length cream chiffon gown with a golden lamé beaded belt with a golden headband with a golden Horus.

With a golden serpent staff.

Lots of gold.

It was the night of the annual Halloween Dance, and I was waiting outside Raritan Hall for Erick to come back with an umbrella of some kind.

It was lightly raining.

I watched as two Vikings, a medieval princess, a crusader, and a George Washington laughingly rushed through the light drizzle into the brightly-lit entrance.

Then I saw him coming.

Riding into my life.

He was riding towards me on a glistening black stallion with a white star between its eyes. He wore all black. With a black Stetson. He was dressed as a westerner, a cowboy, a ranch hand, a gunman without a gun.

But it wasn't a costume.

I knew exactly who he was.

My cousin Erick had told me all about him.

Slowly, he made his way towards me, looking rather magnificent, then he stopped at my buggy. He looked down at me, smiled politely, and spoke.

Reciting.

"The barge she sat in, like a burnish'd throne."

He clearly knew who I was, and, yes, I knew who he was, and I laughed.

"I see Mr. Shakespeare has made his way into the far reaches of distant Arizona."

"All thirty-seven plays," he assured me.

Then he reconsidered.

"Or is it thirty-eight?"

I laughed again.

"Do you often sit on your horse in the rain?" I kidded.

"We like rain in Arizona."

"Fine. When you dry off, why don't you ask me to dance?"

"I just might do that."

Then he smiled, adding:

"Or, then again, I might not."

When my cousin Erick had told me about his new roommate, I was naturally curious. Naturally interested. He told me everything he knew, except for one thing.

"Is he handsome?" I wondered.

"Yes."

Unfortunately, men never elaborate about such things, but now I knew.

I was infatuate.

I was probably already in love.

Later we danced to "The Blue Danube."

Apparently, they can learn to dance the waltz west of the Mississippi.

And learn it well.

To be honest, I don't remember very much. I remember laughing a lot, even though he didn't say that much, unlike most men who seem to be talking all the time about nothing much at all. I remember his politeness, his smile, the way he held me when we danced, the way he looked at me when we talked.

Later, out on the balcony, the rain had stopped, and we were all alone. He took my hand. Needless to say, I was shocked, but I let it happen. Then he looked into my eyes, and he kissed me on the mouth. Now I was *more* than shocked! I was also confused. Yes, it was perfectly lovely, but I didn't know how I should act.

I didn't even know how I *wanted* to act.

"Is that how young men behave where you come from?" I heard myself ask, seemingly with more astonishment than accusation.

"No."

That's all he said.

"No."

"I suppose," I said, "I should have slapped your face and called for Erick to take me home."

"Go ahead."

He was smiling, kidding.

He knew I was going nowhere.

"How was it?" he asked.

I told the truth.

"Lovely."

Then I made an attempt to explain myself.

"I've never been kissed before."

"Well, I've never kissed anyone before."

Which seemed highly unlikely.

"Is that true, Jack?"

"Yes. I *always* tell the truth."

I didn't know what to make of that either.

"Why me?" I asked.

"You know why."

He was right. I *did* know why. At least, I thought I did. I believed that he felt that he loved me the same way that I felt that I loved him. Which was all way too fast, but with inexplicable depth, with unsaid promise.

"I want you to take me to Arizona," I said recklessly, which seemed to come from nowhere.

"Why?"

"To see if there's anyone prettier than me."

It was a terribly vain thing to say, but after all, I was saying it to a terribly forward young man.

"Fine," he decided.

"Then kiss me again."

Which he did.

Promptly.

Perfectly.

[Jennifer Cameron]

Editor's Summary

Sunday, November 11th

According to various newspaper accounts (more specifically the Tucson *Daily Citizen*, the *Tombstone Epitaph*, the Tucson *Arizona Gazette*, the Phoenix *Arizona Star*, etc.), the well-known Mexican pistolero Luis Rodriquez and two accomplices rode into Sasabe early Sunday morning and met with Ethan Cortez, the town mayor, at his home. A verbal confrontation concerning a land purchase ensued, during which Rodriquez mentioned, "It's your last chance, Cortez," and the mayor was overheard saying, "I told you to stay out of this town," and "You can tell Cartas that no one will sell him a square inch of this valley!"

Domingo Cartas was a wealthy Mexican rancher and land baron over the border in Los Tajitos.

Rodriquez immediately left with his men.

Previously, the Mexican gunman had been involved in a number of violent crimes along the southern border, in which at least six people had been killed. Rodriquez, who always wears a red bandido sash at his waist, over his cartridge belt, has been incarcerated several times both in Mexico and the territory, but he's always been quickly released for a variety of nefarious reasons.

Later that morning, the mayor and his wife and their children, two young girls in their Sunday dresses, arrived at the small adobe church, *Capilla del Espiritu Santo*, which served the local Anglos, as well as the Mexicans and the Catholicized Indians. Outside the church, Rodriquez stood waiting near a hitching post with his two companions. He was apparently smoking a cigarette, and he stared at the family with "a look of disdainful amusement." The mayor ignored the man and ushered his family inside the small church.

What happened next was reported by several latecomers, as well as Jason Rawlins, a stable hand at Jensen's Corral. Once the service had begun, during the singing of the hymn "Come Holy Ghost, Creator Blest," Rodriquez walked over to a wooden crate that seemed abandoned at the side of the road near a feeding trough. Then he lifted up the crate and tossed it aside. It was concealing a small detonation pump. Rodriquez flicked his cigarette away, looked coldly at the church, then pressed down on the pump handle. Immediately, the small church exploded in an orgy of cacophonous destruction. It was perfectly clear that Rodriquez and his men had previously rigged the church with mining charges. Probably the night before. The small church was completely destroyed.

Satisfied, Rodriquez and his associates rode away toward the southern border.

Twenty-eight were reported dead in the rubble, including twelve children.

The tragedy is yet another territorial disgrace, further blackening the reputation of Arizona in the eyes of the rest of the country and the rest of the world.

Chapter 7

Birthday

Friday, December 12th

I was getting worried.

I was standing on the back porch waiting for Jack to arrive. Finally, he rode up the darkened street on Night, dressed in a handsome dark blue suit with a dark blue vest.

"I was worried," I said.

He seemed surprised. He pulled up next to me, still sitting on Night, and looked down into my eyes.

"I was worried," I explained foolishly, "that you might not come."

"But I told you that I'd come."

He took out his time piece.

"Right on time," he pointed out. "Eight o'clock."

He was right, of course. I guess I was overly concerned. My parents liked Jack quite a bit, but they remained ambivalent about our relationship.

What would ever come of it?

Did it make any sense?

Etc.

But I was their only daughter, a bit spoiled and raised to be independent, and they knew that any decisions about my future would be my own.

Would I end up in some faraway place called Arizona?

It was hard for them to fathom.

It was even hard for me to fathom.

Even though it seemed like such an exciting possibility.

Jack dismounted, took a small present from his saddlebag, and stepped onto the porch. Then he held me close and whispered, "Happy Birthday."

"Can we just stay out here all night?" I said, even though I knew that everyone was waiting for me inside.

He smiled and held me for a while.

I know this sounds a bit mushy, but I was a young woman and he was a young man, and it's hard to remember such a romance in any other way but romantically.

Later at my party, I made a silent wish and blew out the nineteen candles. I wished, no surprise, that we'd be together forever. Everyone applauded.

It was a lovely party.

All of my best girlfriends were there, as was Erick (you), along with some Rutgers friends, some of my music students, and numerous Cameron family relatives. Not to mention a few administrators and professors from Rutgers where my father served as dean. As for Jack, he really didn't mix that much, but he was always polite and pleasant.

Often I would notice him off to the side, not awkwardly, but definitely at a remove. Eventually, after my mother insisted that I perform Mozart's Fantasia in D Minor, which I did fairly decently, I saw Jack talking with Professor Austin, and I made my way over to listen in. They were obviously talking about Jack's September confrontation with the congressman.

"Sometimes a man needs to speak his mind," Jack said.

Austin, a native Tennessean, was clearly sympathetic and tended to agree.

"When I was a boy, I heard a lot of foolish nonsense about Tennessee. I still do sometimes."

Jack understood and nodded.

"But I'll never," the professor kidded, "bring another politician into my classroom!"

Then Erick and two of his friends joined the group as Austin got a bit more reflective.

"Tell me, John, was Huxley's characterization of the territory so totally inaccurate?"

Concerned, I slipped my arm through Jack's and waited.

"John Ringo was shot in the head three years ago while he was sleeping, Luke Short's left Tombstone for Texas, and Doc Holliday's lungs are dying in Colorado. Morgan Earp is dead, Virgil Earp is crippled for life in California, and Wyatt Earp is a washed-up wanderer searching for gold in Idaho Territory."

He looked closely at the professor and smiled.

"Except for Luke Short, all of them were born east of Texas."

The professor smiled, and Jack continued.

"Most of the people in Arizona are God-fearing men and women, who live in small towns and have never even seen a gunman. Almost all of the publicized violence took place in dying boomtowns like Tombstone, which attracted all kinds of vagrant criminals."

Now that Jack had made his point, I changed the subject.

I lifted my champagne glass and toasted the Rutgersmen.

"To a happy Christmas, then success in all your exams!"

Everyone raised his glass, Jack touched his glass to mine, and we drank my birthday champagne.

But it still wasn't over.

One of the Rutgers sophomores, a young man named Lewis Carter, asked Jack a very reasonable question. One that I'd asked myself.

"What about the Indians, Jack?"

It was a subject that I knew was extremely important to Jack.

"I share my valley and my land with Tohono O'odham, known as Papagos, who are as civilized and Christian as anyone in this room."

It seemed a rather shocking statement, but no one said a word.

"Even the Apaches," Jack continued, "who've survived for centuries by a cruel system of raiding and plunder, being the enemies of every other tribe they've ever encountered, yet even the Apaches are making progress since the surrender of Geronimo. They're smart, courageous, and they'll make a future for themselves eventually."

He wasn't finished.

"All of our problems are far from solved, but law and order has come to Arizona, and statehood is inevitable."

Erick agreed and addressed his professor.

"Sir, did you know that Jack's older brother is currently the territory's Attorney General and that he's running for congressional delegate?"

This clearly interested the professor, and he lifted his glass.

"Well, here's to his success!"

Jack was grateful, but he turned to me instead and held up his glass.

"And here's to the birthday girl!"

It was a wonderful night.

One that I'll never forget.

Experienced back then, and remembered now, through a young lover's eyes.

Mine.

After everyone had left the party, Jack and I returned to the porch alone. I opened his gift. It was a golden chain with a small golden cross.

Beautiful.

Crafted from Arizona gold.

I held him, and I kissed him.

He held me and kissed me back.

Like the young lovers that we were back then.

[Jennifer Cameron]

Editor's Note

Arizona Territory:

Arizona Territory was originally the western region of New Mexico Territory. In 1853, in consequence of the Gadsden Purchase, Arizona was extended further south to a new border with Mexico. It now included Tucson, as well as areas that would later become Yuma and Tombstone.

As early as 1857, Arizona appealed to the US Congress to be recognized as an independent territory. The proposal was defeated in both the House and the Senate. The main reason cited was population scarcity. The 1860 census claimed a population of 6,500 whites, 4,000 Indians, and twenty-one freed Negroes. But that was a bogus excuse. No one had any doubt that the population would increase in time, as with every other territory in the United States. The real reason was concerns in the North about the influence of Southern sympathizers in the region. They were naturally concerned that Arizona would end up a slave territory and eventually a slave state.

When the Civil War broke out, the Confederacy claimed Arizona for the South. Confederate forces under Colonel John Baylor seized Fort Fillmore, declaring Arizona for the Confederacy. The following year, 1862, the US House of Representatives, now controlled by Republicans, passed a bill creating the United States Arizona Territory. The bill was signed by President Abraham Lincoln the following year, and Arizona was now officially its own territory, although its loyalties were still divided until the end of the war.

In 1871 there was an early push for statehood, which happened again when John C. Fremont served as the governor of the territory. Now, of course, the primary issue of contention against Arizona statehood was the widely-reported violence of Apache raids and the bloodshed in the mining boomtowns like Tombstone. It was extremely difficult to undo the image of Tucson as reported by J. Ross Browne, famous author and traveler, who visited the town in 1864 and wrote in *Harper's Magazine* and elsewhere that Tucson was a "paradise of devils," that it was like "what Sodom and Gomorrah must have been before they were destroyed by the vengeance of the Lord." He characterized the inhabitants as "traders, speculators, gamblers, horse-thieves, murderers, and vagrant politicians."

Four years ago, the bloody incident at the O.K. Corral reinforced that image, as it was reported in gory detail in newspapers all over the country and even overseas.

In the year 1885, the possibility of Arizona statehood seemed highly tenuous.

II.

1885

Editor's Summary

Thursday, January 22nd

According to various newspaper accounts, the ruthless bank robber Richard Brady, accompanied by two heavily-armed associates, rode into Globe, Arizona, yesterday morning. It was an overcast Thursday in Globe, a silver mining town now shifting to copper. The three men dismounted in front of the small branch of Central Arizona Bank and entered carrying shotguns. There were only a few patrons in the bank at the time along with a bank clerk, Abraham Jayson, and the branch manager, Elisha Holt.

According to witnesses, Brady immediately walked behind the counter to the desk of the bank manager, who began to say, "You can't come in," before he was smashed in the face with the butt of Brady's shotgun. Brady, a large, violent, pock-marked man with a dark moustache, forced the bleeding Holt over to the safe and demanded that he open it. When Holt bravely refused to do so, Brady went back around the counter and apprehended a young woman, Lisabeth Curry, a local homesteader's wife of twenty-five. Grabbing her by the hair, he forced her back to Holt and the bank safe. Mrs. Curry, similarly displaying remarkable courage, was clearly frightened yet not hysterical.

As Holt watched in horror, Brady struck Mrs. Curry in the face. Then he reached under his long black dress-coat and pulled out a leather saddle cord which he quickly wrapped around the helpless woman's neck. As he stared at Holt, Brady began to strangle the woman. Terrified, Holt immediately conceded, mumbling, "All right! All right!" as he began working the safe's combination. But even after he'd opened the safe, Brady continued to strangle the young woman until she fell limp, clearly dead, with bulged blue eyes.

"You'll pay for this," Holt said angrily.

"By whom?" Brady responded dismissively.

"We have a good sheriff in this town!"

"Where?"

Suddenly concerned, Mr. Holt said nothing more.

Brady looked over at his two men and said, "Get the money and find me." He immediately left the bank and walked up the Main Street to the sheriff's office. Inside, Ed Sheridan, a young deputy, was sitting at his desk reading the day's newspaper. Brady pushed the newspaper away with the barrel of his shotgun.

"Where's the sheriff?"

Sheridan said nothing.

Then Sheriff Alexander Dawson entered the room asking, "Can I help you, sir?" Richard Brady turned around and emptied both shells into the man's chest. Dawson, a reputable sheriff, age fifty-four, died instantly.

When Brady stepped outside, his accomplices rode up the street with his horse. Then they rode out of town at a leisurely pace.

Richard Brady, age forty-five, wanted for numerous crimes, is known to have robbed banks and/or coach transports in Bisbee, Winslow, Kingman, and Nogales.

Probably more.

Chapter 8

Bookstore

Thursday, January 15th

It was curious.

Especially now that I think back on it.

It was a pleasant day in mid-January, and I went over to Baxter's Books & Readings on Albany Street, as I did every other Thursday. I remember that I was wearing a dark green woolen overcoat that day, over a light-green dress beneath a light-green poke bonnet. I'd already collected a few titles and was happily browsing alone down one of the aisles.

I was relaxed and enjoying myself.

"Jennifer."

I knew who it was immediately, but I was a bit startled anyway. I turned around to see Jack, western-dressed in black, looking a bit out of place in the best bookstore in New Brunswick.

"Jack," I said stupidly before regaining my composure. "I thought you were studying for exams?"

I learned later that Jack had spotted me from the front window of the post office on Albany Street, where he was picking up his mail from out west, which was usually a pile of newspaper clippings forwarded by someone with the colorful name of Texas Jim Ellis.

Despite my surprise to see him in the bookstore, I was still happy to see him of course, despite the mischievous look on his face. It seemed obvious that he was suspicious of something and that he'd decided to have a little fun with me.

"So what's the music teacher reading these days?" he asked.

I shifted the books in my hands and held out three.

The *Oresteia*, Marcus Aurelius (which Jack had recommended), and the correspondence of John Adams (which Jack had also recommended).

He was clearly pleased, but still curious.

"And the others?"

"Oh, just some light reading," I explained, putting him off as best I could.

He held out his hand.

I placed the three little books in his hand, and he read the titles.

Was I embarrassed?

I suppose I was.

He looked them over more closely.

All were Beadle's Dime Novels, of the "frontier" and "western" variety. Not exactly the most elevated reading, although they were, of course, incredibly popular. Each book, as you know, was a potboiler, titillating, superficial, sensationalized, and concocted to incite the passions.

Jack looked them over as if they'd come from another planet.

The Blue Rider of New Mexico.
Billy Bonney's Last Showdown.
The Tucson Kid Tames Tombstone.

Not exactly Aeschylus, but I have to admit, I found them irresistible.

Jack stared intently at the cover sketches of sinister gunmen and wild shootouts.

He looked at me.

"*The Tucson Kid Tames Tombstone?*"

He was having his fun.

"Well, Mr. Shannon, I happen to like them," I said a bit too defensively.

Oddly, he seemed concerned about something, and I realized what was bothering him.

"Don't worry, Jack, I would never confuse fantasy with reality. I love Jack Shannon not the Blue Rider of New Mexico."

"Good, because there aren't any Blue Riders of New Mexico."

I understood.

Perfectly.

"I've read these little books ever since I was a young girl, Jack. There needs to be a break sometimes between the Greeks and Mr. Adams."

But Jack was now staring down at a wooden bookshelf where I'd placed another title that I'd been considering. He picked it up. The title was *Retribution Finds the Arizona Gunmen.*

"Maybe I should get that one too," I kidded.
"Maybe you've got enough already."
Which seemed an odd thing to say.
Then he put it back on the shelf.

[Jennifer Cameron]

Editor's Summary

Thursday, April 7th

According to various newspaper accounts, the notorious shootist Damien Stark arrived in Benson the previous night, keeping to himself at the Benson Hotel. Eventually word of his arrival circulated around the small terminal town established five years ago by the Southern Pacific Railroad, twenty-five miles from Tombstone.

The next morning around nine o'clock, Stark was observed smoking a cigarette, leaning against the wooden side wall of the mercantile in a narrow alleyway near the main street in town. Damien Stark is reputed to be thirty-two years old and believed to have killed at least seven men throughout the territory as well as several over the border in Mexico. Lean, tall, and clean-shaven, Stark wore a dark black suit over a grey cotton shirt with a black Texas tie, beneath a black Stetson. He carries a Cavalry Model Peacemaker with a 7½-inch barrel in his right-side leather holster. He's known to be extremely deadly. Extremely proficient. In more than one newspaper report, he's been claimed to be "the most dangerous gunman in the Arizona territory."

Or, sometimes, "the most formidable."

In the bright morning sunshine, he was waiting for his prey.

Completely unaware, Judge Jonathan Dolan and US Marshal Charles Caldwell came up the street talking pleasantly on the bright April morning. Caldwell was a reputable and confident man in his early forties, and the judge is said to be fifty-five, unmarried, and unarmed.

Neither man noticed Stark until he emerged from the alleyway and intercepted their path. Everyone else immediately cleared the street.

"What do *you* want?" Caldwell asked sternly.

"Retribution."

Which seemed rather peculiar.

"Don't be foolish, Stark," the marshal warned him.

"Retribution for what?" the judge asked with obvious irritation.

Stark said nothing. He just stared coldly at the judge.

"Leave the judge out of it," Caldwell warned him.

But Stark ignored him and continued to stare at the judge. Finally, he answered the man's question.

"Surely you remember my cousin Luke Strong?"

"Yes, but we do our best to forget scum like that," the judge responded.

Defiantly.

Two months earlier, Judge Dolan had sentenced Luke Strong to hang in Tucson after the man had killed two drovers during a botched rustling attempt southwest of the city.

Concerned for the judge's well-being, the marshal stepped to his left away from the judge.

Did he really believe that he had a chance against a man like Damien Stark? It's impossible to know. But he certainly knew his duty.

His sense of honor.

Stark drew and fired twice. No other shots were fired. The first bullet blew a hole through the marshal's heart and the other struck the judge in the forehead. Both immediately collapsed to the street, stirring up dust.

Stark stepped forward, stared down at both men, and when he was satisfied, he holstered his weapon. Then he walked back to the alleyway, untethered his Morgan, and rode out of Benson.

A few months earlier, a pathetic councilman in the capital city of Prescott had actually suggested paying Stark a sizable sum to leave the territory. "Let's send him to Texas. Or maybe Mexico." Which was yet another in a long string of embarrassments for Arizona Territory.

Chapter 9

Long Branch

Saturday, April 25th

"**I**'ve never had a second one before!"

We'd just finished dining, open-air, oceanfront, on the back patio of the Scarboro Hotel in popular Long Branch on the New Jersey coast, and I'd ordered a second glass of champagne. Off to my left, as the twilight fell, was the ocean pier, the active casino, and the brightly colored lights of the amusement park. Long Branch was the most fashionable resort in America, attracting wealthy New Yorkers like Diamond Jim Brady; theatrical stars like Lillian Russell, Edwin Booth, and Lily Langtry; and even the past four presidents, one of whom, the tragic Garfield, had died right here in Long Branch after his assassination in Washington, DC.

That evening as I sipped at my second glass of white champagne, I was wearing my prettiest whitest frilliest dress with a matching parasol. I felt quite marvelous, as if I sparkled myself. I suppose I was feeling the effects of the champagne, enjoying our special trip to the coast before

Jack left for home in about two weeks. I was doing my best to put such thoughts out of my mind and the bubbles were helping.

"Two glasses of champagne!" I said, holding up my glass. "I believe it's making me silly!"

Jack smiled. He was dressed to the nines in a custom navy three-piece, and he reached across the small table and held my hand.

"You're beautiful, Jennifer, with or without champagne."

Which I liked very much.

Then he looked at the dark endless Atlantic.

"I've never seen an ocean before."

I'd never thought about that before.

"So what do you think?" I kidded.

"Marvelous."

"Which do you prefer to look at?" I asked.

Which I *really* did ask!

I hope you can forgive my honesty and my silliness, but I was definitely a little bit "lit" by the champagne, and underneath everything I was terrified that I was going to lose him.

Jack, of course, gave the correct answer.

"You, of course."

"Do you really need to leave for the summer, Jack?"

He leaned towards me and looked into my eyes.

"I'll be back, Jennifer."

I believed him.

Later we were walking the walkway near the pier. I was a bit tipsy for the first time in my life, but definitely enjoying myself, holding on to Jack. Tightly. As we strolled into the amusement park, near a shooting gallery, we heard a familiar voice.

"Jack! Jennifer!"

It was you, Erick, along with two other Rutgers boys, accompanied by two New Brunswick girls, all of whom we knew quite well. They were standing at one of those shooting galleries that advertises: "5 Shots At 5 Candles, 3 Wins A Prize." Standing at the counter, Lewis Carter was taking his last, slow, careful aim at one of the four lit candles. He fired and missed badly, but he turned around rather pleased with himself.

"Well, I got one of them!"

"Damned lucky!" Erick kidded.

I'd never heard Erick use a work like that, but they'd obviously been drinking as well.

After all, it was Long Branch!

"You're right about that," Lewis admitted.

Then Erick turned to Jack.

"Why don't you give it a try, Jack?"

It wasn't really a challenge, more of a friendly persuasion, and everyone was clearly intrigued by the possibility.

Including me.

How would a real westerner do with a gun in his hand?

Jack said nothing.

"What do you say, Jack?" Lewis prompted.

Jack looked at me.

I nodded.

"Please."

I suppose that Jack, at that moment, decided that it might be best for me to witness some of the hidden truth about himself.

Without another word, he walked up to the rail and placed a coin on the counter. Then he looked down at the handgun and smiled. He picked it up and studied it carefully, quickly. Deftly, he examined its firing pin, removed the cylinder, checked the cartridges, and looked down the barrel. Then he reassembled the gun, removing two of the cartridges and replacing them with two others from the counter. I was fascinated. I believe everyone else was as well.

Finally, Jack looked at the old proprietor who'd now relit the fifth candle.

"Not much of a piece," Jack kidded.

The old boy smiled and shrugged.

"But not the worst either."

Then Jack placed another coin down on the counter.

"For a test," he said to the old man.

This confused me a bit, even more so when Jack raised his weapon and fired a round into the corner of the wooden booth at no discernable target.

But he seemed satisfied.

Then he took a step back from the railing, held the revolver at his right side, and glanced at the five lit candles arranged in a rising diagonal from left to right.

He turned to me.

"What do you think?"

By which, maybe he meant, "How many do you think I'll blow out?" but I wasn't sure. When he turned back, the gun rose and fired five rapid staccato shots, as the five candle lights extinguished in an almost simultaneous progression. Then Jack stepped through the gunpowder smoke and placed the weapon back on the counter.

Needless to say, everyone was stunned

Jack turned back to me, took my hand, and led me up to the counter and pointed to all the prizes.

"Take your pick."

I picked a stuffed fluffy white bear, still not certain if I'd actually seen what I'd actually seen.

Later we were sitting on the deck of the *Jersey Comfort*, a leisure boat that was slowly cruising along the coastline close to the shore at Long Branch, not far from the beach, not far from all the elegant hotels, not far from the illuminated pier and the amusement park.

Yes, it had been one of the most marvelous days of my life, but the lingering problem was still there, of course, lurking at the back of my mind. To distract myself, I asked Jack about something else.

"I'd like to watch," I said.

"Watch what?" he asked, although I think he knew what I meant. What I wanted.

"I want to watch you practice."

As he thought it over, I pressed him.

"Surely, you practice, Jack."

He'd seen me play the piano, and he knew that I knew something about practice.

He nodded yes.

"I thought you boys," I kidded, "weren't allowed to have guns at Rutgers."

He smiled and decided.

"All right, Jennifer. It might be better that way."

I didn't ask him what he meant by that, but I think I knew.

Then he changed the subject.

"Did you know that William Harris came from Long Branch?"

"William Harris? Who's that?"

He gave me his "Jack" smile.

"Surely you've read about him in your dime novels."

"Sorry, smart aleck, but I don't remember the name."

"William Harris moved to Dodge City, Kansas, bought a saloon, and renamed it the Long Branch Saloon after his hometown."

"I had no idea," I admitted.

It was the first time that Jack had talked to me about that aspect of the West, about anything relating to guns or gunfights. I had no idea, of course, that the most famous and most notorious saloon in the West, once associated with Wyatt Earp, Bat Masterson, Doc Holliday, Luke Short, and others, got its name from Long Branch, New Jersey, and I think Jack told me just to please me.

To make me happy.

Which it did.

"Luke Short," he added, "later became a part-owner of the Long Branch."

"I had no idea," I repeated.

But it did make me curious about something else, even though I should have known better.

Maybe it was the champagne, which, I guess, is getting blamed for everything.

"Does Mr. Jack Shannon read the Beadle books?" I kidded.

"Never, Miss Cameron."

So I snuggled closer to my love in the cooling night, and he pulled the deck blanket up to my waist.

"It's been a wonderful day, Jack," I admitted, "but I still worry."

"Don't, a summer only lasts so long."

"I know. I know."

Then he looked out over the water and pointed at an isolated light on the shore.

"I think that's it."

"Grant's house?"

"Yes."

We'd been looking for it.

Like everyone else in the country we knew that the great general and president was dying of cancer at his home in Long Branch. He was also writing his memoirs.

"My father met him once," Jack said.

I was amazed.

"Tell me."

"He was consulted about Indian affairs in New Mexico Territory, which once included Arizona. My father took the train east, and they met at the White House. My father greatly admired the man about many things, but especially his attempts to establish a humane policy regarding the western Indian tribes. The government had made and broken over 370 previous treaties with the various tribes, and President Grant did his best to foster reconciliation and fairness."

Again, for the first time, Jack was talking about the West. About his home. About something that meant a great deal to him since I knew that he shared his ranch with members of the Papago Indian tribe.

He continued.

"Grant once said that 'All citizens undoubtedly in all respects should be equal.' Which was something that not very many people agreed with."

"Well," I agreed, "he certainly did his best, against all kinds of opposition, for southern Blacks. I read somewhere that Frederick Douglas called him 'our shelter in the storms of the past.'"

"Yes, and Douglas also said, as my father was fond of quoting, 'To Grant more than any other man the Negro owes his enfranchisement and the Indian a humane policy.'"

But now that great man, the most famous and admired man in the world, was dying not far away in his seaside cottage. It was very sad to think about, but we were suddenly startled by a loud blast from the shore at the pier.

I sat up excitedly.

"It's starting, Jack!"

Immediately, with loud cacophony, rockets shot upwards into the night and the dark skies over the shoreline were filled with a spectacular shower of red, white, green, and blue fireworks explosions.

It was marvelous.

It was breathtaking.

Brilliant.

Jack held me close and when I looked into his eyes, which were now lit with the fireworks' colored lights, he kissed me.

Or I kissed him.

Then he whispered.

Softly.

"I'll be back, Jennifer."

So you've asked me about these things, and I've told you the way I've remembered it. As best I can. I don't care if these memories seem like the fancies of an infatuate young girl because I *was* an infatuate young girl, and they were *not* fancies.

It was real.

Very real.

[Jennifer Cameron]

Chapter 10

Raritan

Monday, May 4th

I didn't know what was going on, but I did it anyway.

As directed, I drove Jennifer in her father's trap down to the Raritan to an abandoned old barnyard and corral. It was a lovely May day, and Jennifer, as always, was lovely, wearing a yellow ruffled dress with matching bonnet.

I pulled the buggy up beside the old corral where Jack was waiting in his western clothes and black Stetson with two obvious additions. A holstered black-butted gun at his right side and another gun tucked under the center of his leather belt. At that point in time, Jack had been my roommate for eight months, and we were very good friends, even best friends, but I'd never seen him looking like that.

He smiled his friendly smile, but he looked rather fearsome.

Even dangerous.

Jennifer said nothing, and I helped her down from the trap. Behind Jack, near the old wooden barn, a young boy about twelve was waiting with a wicker basket, which was, I learned later, filled with "gone bad" apples which he'd purchased from a local grocer earlier this morning.

For target practice.

Jack came over, nodded at me, then looked at Jennifer.

"Miss Cameron," he said politely.

But Jennifer said nothing, staring down at his two handguns.

"Well," Jack explained with a smile, "I can't wear church clothes *all* the time."

She nodded, but Jack still seemed concerned.

"Are you afraid of me, Jennifer?"

"No, never."

"A man needs to be able to defend himself and defend his family. Especially where I come from."

"I know that Jack."

When she'd regained her composure, Jack nodded at a wooden crate which he'd set nearby, and Jennifer sat down. I found a similar crate and sat down as well.

Jennifer nodded at his weapons.

"Tell me about them."

Jack removed the revolver from his holster so she could see it clearly.

"The most popular guns west of the Mississippi are Samuel Colt's revolvers. He created the prototype, known as the "Paterson," right here in New Jersey. This one is a single-action six-shot Colt .45 with a custom 7½-inch barrel."

He held it up.

"The Peacemaker," she said.

"Yes," Jack smiled, "although some people call it the Exterminator."

He handed the weapon to Jennifer.

"It's not loaded," he assured her.

She took it gingerly, with great interest, then looked up at Jack.

"No front sight," she said.

"No front sight," he agreed.

"But what I don't understand is how you can work it so quickly if it's single-action."

I must say, I was rather surprised by Jennifer's apparent knowledge regarding firearms, but then again, my cousin was *always* surprising me. I suppose it was all those silly dime novels she was always devouring.

"You need to cock it with your thumb," Jack explained, "and practice and practice. Until it's nothing more than a reflex."

"How often?"

"I come here five days a week."

Jennifer handed me the Colt, and I looked it over. It was heavier than I expected.

She had more questions.

"Are there *real* gunmen, Jack?"

"Very few, Jennifer. Most men don't carry a gun unless it's necessary. The sheriffs need them, of course, and the guys who drive the herds need them as well, mainly to shoot rattlesnakes, which can kill the cattle. They're also useful when swarding off rustlers."

"But are there *real* gunmen?" she repeated.

"Just a few left. Most are dead, mostly bushwhacked. Besides, the few that can handle a gun seldom confront each other. They tend to give each other a wide berth, although Davis Tutt foolishly faced down Hickok in Springfield, Missouri, and Levi Richardson made the same deadly mistake with Texas Frank Loving in the Long Branch Saloon seven years ago."

"Who were the best?"

"From what I heard from my father and others, a man would be ill-advised to get on the bad side of Ben Thompson or Bill Hickok or Luke Short. Or Doc Holliday, Jim Courtright, John Wesley Hardin, Clay Allison, or Dallas Stoudenmire."

All of whom, except for Hickok and Holliday, were names that I'd never heard of, but it was clear that Jennifer recognized most of them.

"Were they fast or accurate?"

Jack laughed.

"The best ones were both, but keep in mind that at the O.K. Corral, over thirty shots were fired in thirty seconds and most of them missed."

"Who was the fastest?"

"Some would say Luke Short, others would say John Wesley Hardin."

"Are there any gunmen left in Arizona?"

"Just a few."

Behind Jack, about twenty-five yards away, the young boy was placing his targets in various places near the front of the old barn. Some were waist high, some low, some placed up quite a bit higher.

Jennifer pointed at the gun in Jack's belt.

"What about that one?"

"It's my father's old Walker Colt. It's a five-shot advancement on the Paterson which Colt made for the Texas Rangers. For Samuel Walker. It's very heavy with a lot of firepower."

Jack removed the long-barreled gun from his belt and handed it to Jennifer.

"Also unloaded," he added.

She took it and looked up at Jack.

"It feels like a cannon."

"It is. It's the most powerful handgun ever made, but it's a bit of a handful and definitely less accurate that the .45."

When Jennifer passed me the Walker, I handed Jack his Peacemaker, which he quickly loaded then holstered as we talked.

The Walker felt eerily lethal in my hands.

"Ready, sir!" the young boy called out. He was now standing far off to the right of the barn.

I handed Jack his Walker, which he also loaded quickly, then tucked beneath his belt.

Then he looked at the both of us and smiled.

"I guess it's time to pop a few apples."

Immediately, he turned around, drew his .45 and fired six shots in a rapid frenzy all exploding hapless red apples all over the barnyard. Then he pulled out his Walker with his left hand and fired off five more loud rounds. Two of which blew apples out of the air which had been tossed upwards by the young boy. His final shot, however, seemed to miss any target, and a single remaining red apple was still sitting on a railing close to the barn.

Regardless, it was astonishing.

Needless to say.

What other word could I use?

Jack stood motionless within the dissipating cloud of white smoke left by the "black-powder" gunpowder. Then he watched as the young boy ran over to the barn door, bent down, then happily held up a large dead rat by its tail, which was, to be perfectly honest, rather disgusting.

Jack nodded, slid his .45 slowly into his holster then tucked the Walker back under his belt.

He turned around to face us directly.

"The kid," he explained, "gets a dime for every rat we kill on the property."

I said nothing, but Jennifer looked up at Jack.

"Could anybody else do that?"

Meaning, as I understood it, "Could anyone else in the entire world do what we'd just witnessed?"

Jack thought it over, apparently wondering how to answer her question.

Which he did.

"No."

It was that simple.

Then he walked over and sat down on a low railing near the both of us. He knew her questions weren't over, and he'd clearly decided that she deserved to know the answers.

"Why?" she asked.

So he told her.

"When I was a boy, I saw a man gunned down in the street in Tucson, and one of the strays nearly hit my mother. So I went home, and I told my father that I wanted to 'get good' with a handgun. I was only eight at the time, and I believe I said that I wanted to get 'better than anyone.' So he taught me all the basics with his big heavy Walker. No frills, no showy stuff. One holster, a right-side gun, a back-up weapon, proper balance, shoot from the waist, always calm, always practice. Etc."

Jack grew thoughtful, remembering.

"But my father always said that I needed to be proficient, but never so good that I'd develop some kind of reputation. Which he said, 'can get a man killed.' But, of course, I didn't listen."

When Jack hesitated, Jennifer prompted.

"Tell me, Jack."

"After he died, I wanted to be *more* than just proficient. I had no intention of becoming some kind of gunman, but I wanted to be able to protect Rising Sun the best I could. So I went into Tombstone, to Fly's Boarding House, and knocked on John Holliday's door."

We were both amazed.

"Doc?" Jennifer asked.

"Yes, I was fifteen at the time, and I wanted to refine myself, refine my abilities with a gun. When I introduced myself, Doc said that he'd always respected my father, who was one of the most famous ranchers in southern Arizona. I know it's been claimed that Doc Holliday was a gambler, a hot-tempered drunk, a consort of prostitutes, and a cold-blooded killer, all of which was true. But he was also a well-educated Southern gentleman from Georgia, who was dying of tuberculosis, who was nothing but kind to me. So we spent the entire afternoon alone together in his room."

"Doing what?"

"Mostly talking. He asked me to draw once, which I did, and he said there was nothing he needed to add. 'You've been taught just right, young boy,' he said."

"So what did you talk about?"

"Four things. He emphasized that I keep things basic, with nothing done for show, 'even though I myself make that mistake from time to time.'"

"What else?"

"Never let anyone know how good you are. 'Reputation kills, young man. Keep yourself anonymous and only use your skills to protect the ones you love. To protect Rising Sun.'"

"The other two?"

"Doc is ambidextrous, and he told me to develop my left hand, which I've done, making it almost the equal of my right. Lastly, we talked about matters of temperament. He was glad to learn that I'd read Marcus Aurelius closely, and he suggested Lucretius."

Jack looked at Jennifer.

"I learned a lot that day."

He paused again, then continued.

"There's no need for you to worry about me, Jennifer."

Which, I believe, was the whole point of everything that had happened that morning. He loved her, and he wanted her to know the truth about himself, and he also wanted her to know that she had no reason to fear him and no reason to fear *for* him.

And that she would always be safe with him.

At least, that's what I assumed.

It was clear that they both loved each other very much, but I was still worried about it.

Later that night, when I was alone with Jack, I asked him a question of my own.

"Did you ever meet Wyatt Earp?"

"Nope. No thanks. Not interested."

So much for that!

[Erick Ramsey]

Editor's Note

Gunmen, Outlaws:

(A short miscellany of selective facts which Jack Shannon was fond of citing.)

1876 – Wild Bill Hickok shot in the back in Deadwood, Dakota Territory

1878 – John Wesley Hardin sentenced to twenty-five years in Huntsville Prison

1881 – Billy the Kid Bonny killed (ambushed?) by Pat Garrett at Fort Sumner, New Mexico Territory

1882 – Jesse James shot in the back of the head by Robert Ford in St. Joseph, Missouri

1882 – Jim Leavy ambushed by John Murphy in Tucson, Arizona Territory

1882 – Johnny Ringo found dead with a bullet to his right temple in Cochise County, Arizona Territory

1882 – Dallas Stoudenmire killed by the Manning brothers in El Paso, Texas

The O.K. Corral:

Mid-afternoon, Wednesday, October 26, 1881, the long-standing feud in the silver boomtown of Tombstone located in southeast Arizona Territory came to a head with a deadly confrontation at approximately three o'clock. The conflict was incited by a band of local outlaws known collectively as the Cochise County Cowboys, led by the Clanton brothers and the McLaury brothers, who, as they'd done in the past, were in clear violation of the Tombstone ordinance prohibiting the carrying of weapons within the city limits.

The law was represented by Virgil Earp, the Tombstone sheriff who was also a deputy US marshal, along with his two younger deputized brothers Wyatt and Morgan, as well as a hastily deputized associate Doc Holliday. The confrontation took place in a narrow lot (approximately twenty-feet wide) on Fremont Street between the Harwood House and Fly's Boarding House near the O.K. Corral. The four lawmen initially faced six of the Cowboys, at a distance of no more than ten feet apart, but three of the latter, Ike Clanton, Wes Fuller, and Billy Claiborne fled from the scene when the shooting started.

Once Virgil Earp had announced, "Throw up your hands! I want your guns!", it's not perfectly clear who fired first, but it seems most probable that it was Frank McLaury and Billy Clanton. The consequence was a furious exchange of gunfire in which thirty cartridges were fired in no more than a half-minute. When the smoke cleared, Billy Clanton, Frank McLaury, and Tom McLaury were dead. Virgil Earp had been shot through the calf, Morgan Earp was wounded across the back of his shoulders, Doc Holliday was grazed at the hip, and Wyatt Earp was completely unharmed.

In the aftermath, the Earp contingent was completely cleared of any criminality, but the town remained divided between those supporting the local cowboys and those supporting the "outsider" Earps. Two months later, Virgil Earp was ambushed, during which his left arm was seriously damaged, making it essentially useless for the rest of his life. Three months after that, on March 18, 1982, Morgan Earp was shot in the back and killed while playing billiards.

Soon afterwards, Virgil Earp and his wife Allie left Tombstone for his parents' home in Colton, California, but Wyatt Earp formed a deputized federal posse to exact revenge on the Cowboys. He was joined by Doc Holliday and others in what has become known as Wyatt Earp's Vendetta Ride. Over the next few months, Frank Stilwell was killed with a shotgun in Tucson, Charlie Cruz was killed at the South Pass of the Dragoon Mountains, and Wyatt Earp killed Curly Bill Brocius with a shotgun during a shootout near Iron Springs.

In April 1882, since they were under warrants for the death of Frank Stilwell, Earp and Holliday left Arizona Territory and headed north to Colorado.

The O.K. Corral incident was highly publicized and highly sensationalized in newspapers all over the country, as well as overseas. It was yet another bloody episode in the recent history of the Arizona Territory that has been routinely cited by opponents of the territory's application for statehood.

Chapter 11

New Brunswick Train Station

Tuesday, May 12th

I shook Jack's hand.

Then I stepped back on the platform.

The train was waiting, steaming up the train station.

Jack, in his navy travel suit, stood with Jennifer on the platform. She was dressed in white, looking lovely, doing her best to be brave.

She handed Jack her small going-away present.

He was uncertain if he was supposed to open it, so she let him know.

"Yes."

Jack removed the blue ribbon and the white wrapping paper. It was a black bandana. Surely an expensive one, purchased in New York City.

Jack was obviously pleased.

"Do you like it?" she asked to be certain.

Jack nodded that he did, then he handed her the ribbon and the paper, so he could tie the bandana around his neck, which was oddly incongruous with his traveling clothes.

The whistle blasted.

They knew it was almost time.

He stepped closer, kissed her on the mouth, and she fell into his arms. He held her tightly, as she buried her face into his chest.

The distant voice of the conductor could be heard.

"All aboard!"

Jennifer looked up into his eyes.

Sadly.

"I'll be back," he said softly.

Then he nodded over at me, as if to say, "Take care of her, Erick." As if to say, "Take care of your cousin."

Then, as the train slowly began to move, he stepped from the platform onto the train, turned around, and was soon lost in the enveloping steam.

Jennifer stood alone, similarly shrouded in white mist.

It hurt my heart in multiple ways, so I stepped over and put my arm around her.

To comfort her.

"He'll be back," I said, with as much conviction as I could muster.

What else could I say?

[Erick Ramsey]

Chapter 12

Prescott

Monday, May 18th

He came down from the train.

He looked a bit like his older brother. His half-brother. He was taller, trimmer, and twelve years younger, but I could still see the resemblance. He looked quite handsome in his dark travel suit, with his dark hair, with his dark eyes. I suspect that young women would find him very appealing. He was definitely more, how shall I put it?, "rugged" than his older brother, which made perfect sense given that, despite a year at college, he was still a rancher and Edward was always a lawyer. A civil servant.

"Welcome, young man!" I said as I extended my hand.

We shook.

He'd sent me a telegram last night from Albuquerque letting me know about his arrival in Prescott and his plan to surprise his older brother.

I was happy to oblige.

He carried a small overnight bag, and I looked around for the rest.

"I've made arrangements," he explained, "for my horse and the rest of my baggage. I'm planning to stay in Prescott for two or three days."

He had a confident competent air about him, but nothing arrogant. As a matter of fact, he was quite polite, respectful of me and my age (I was fifty-two at the time), and very pleasant.

We'd never met before, but I'd served as Edward's advisor and associate for the past eight years, and I'd heard a good deal about Jack Shannon, and I'm sure that he'd heard a few things about me as well.

At the end of the platform, the young man stopped to look over the capital city, centered around the Territorial Courthouse, located in the foothills of the Mazatzal Mountains. It was still early morning, and the town was gradually coming alive. Nearby two station workers were hoisting an American flag over the train station, and Jack watched respectfully. Then he noticed a large campaign sign nailed to the side of the train station.

It read:

SHANNON MEANS STATEHOOD!

And smaller:

VOTE SHANNON!

Jack turned to me.

"Is he going to win this thing?"

He was referring to the upcoming election for Territorial Delegate to the House of Representatives. The position didn't include voting rights, but it was, except for governor, the most important position in the territory, especially regarding the application for statehood. Edward had done an excellent job as the state's Attorney General, and now he was determined to go to Washington and lobby for Arizona.

I answered honestly.

"It's close, Jack. Very close."

"Is he ahead or behind?"

"I'd say a bit behind at this point."

Actually, maybe he was more than just "a bit" behind.

Later, when I was stopped by a colleague in the courthouse lobby, Jack went over to stare at the various "WANTED" notices that were posted on one of the lobby's bulletin boards.

He removed three.

Which seemed rather odd.

Then I led him upstairs to his brother's office.

When we entered, Edward was sitting at his desk. When he looked up from his papers, he was both delighted and surprised.

"Jack! I can't believe it!"

He rose immediately from his seat, came around the desk, and warmly shook his brother's hand.

Then he looked at me.

"Why didn't you let me know, Phil?"

He wasn't displeased, just curious.

"He wanted to surprise you," I explained.

"Well, he certain has!"

Then he gestured to the two chairs facing his desk, and Jack and I sat down.

Edward sat back on his desk.

"It's so good to see you, Jack!"

"It's good to see you."

"We'll celebrate tonight! But first, tell me all about the east coast? How was Rutgers?"

"Just fine, Edward."

I'd been told that Jack was a bit laconic, but "just fine" seemed excessively so.

Edward was undaunted.

He smiled.

"Any special Eastern women?"

Jack just smiled. Then he stood up and changed the subject.

"Mr. Whitson tells me you might lose the election. Do you feel the same way?"

Edward suddenly turned serious.

"Philip is a very honest man, and it's certainly close. Jason Mitchell's quite popular and well-connected."

"Is he crooked?"

We were both surprised by the question, but Edward did his best to be truthful.

"I don't know, Jack, but there've been rumors."

There was subsequent silence.

Until the kid broke it.

"Why haven't there been more arrests?"

It was an intractable problem that Edward and I had been dealing with for a long time.

"It's a good question, Jack. Philip and I discuss it all the time. I guess I'd blame it mostly on local politics and lazy marshals."

Which seemed to be what the young man was expecting to hear.

He stepped closer to his brother's desk.

"I've come with a purpose, Edward, and I'd like you to listen."

Edward seemed as surprised as I was that his younger brother had an interest in politics, but he was clearly willing to listen.

Since I wasn't sure if I should stay, I stood up.

"Maybe I should leave."

But Edward was insistent.

"No, Phil, please stay."

Then he looked at his brother.

"We have no secrets," he explained. "I trust Philip with my life."

Jack seemed fine with my involvement.

When he nodded, I sat down, and Jack explained his intentions.

"At sundown, on Tuesday, July 7th, I plan to bring into Prescott, all alive, Richard Stark, Richard Brady, and Luis Rodriquez."

Needless to say, the Attorney General and I were stunned.

Stunned and incredulous.

During that moment of incredulity, Jack pulled out the three "WANTED" posters from his jacket and placed them on the desk in front of his brother.

He continued.

"I believe they can be arraigned, tried, and hung within two weeks' time. Then on Tuesday, July 28th, you'll win the election for congressional delegate."

We were still in shock.

"You can't be serious, Jack."

Even though the kid didn't respond, his demeanor made it perfectly clear that he was deadly serious.

I looked at Edward.

"Could he really do such a thing?" I asked, probably foolishly, after all the kid was only twenty years old.

Edward dismissed the idea.

"Of course not! He'll get himself killed!"

But the kid spoke again.

Both serious and final.

"I *will* be doing it, Edward. Regardless of your opinions and concerns. I came here today to let you know what I intend to do, and to secure the legal authority, including documents with the power to deputize."

"Deputize whom?" Edward asked a bit irritated.

"Who do you think?"

It was perfectly clear that Edward knew who Jack meant, but I had no idea that it was a young Indian named John Red Star.

"I don't think they should be involved," Edward said, without clarifying.

"Why not? They live in Arizona like the rest of us."

Edward had no response.

He grew quiet and pensive, then he backed around his desk and sat down in his chair again. He was clearly concerned. Worried. He looked over at his brother.

"I think you'll be killed, Jack."

"You've been away from Rising Sun for over ten years. I'm much better than you have any idea."

Which also wasn't perfectly clear.

Which wasn't said as a reproach, but as a fact.

Edward thought it over.

"Can I talk you out of it?" he tried.

"No."

It was clear that one thing the half-brothers had in common was stubbornness.

Edward tried again.

"We're talking about the three most wanted men in the entire territory."

"Exactly."

Then Edward tried a different tact, trying to be reasonable.

"At least leave Stark out of this. He's much too dangerous."

"They're all dangerous."

"But Stark is different. I'm told that he's better than John Wesley Hardin."

The kid was unperturbed.

"I want Stark myself," he said.

Then he added, "And he wants me."

Naturally, Edward was surprised.

"Do you know the man?"

"We've never met."

A bit flummoxed, as was I, Edward sat back in his chair and reconsidered. He could see his brother's inflexible resolve, and he knew that he could never sway him from his intended purpose. Finally, he made a decision.

"All right, Jack, I'll do whatever you want, and I'll give you whatever you need."

The kid was pleased.

"There's one more thing, Edward. I want my name kept out of it."

He looked over at me and stated the obvious.

"Only three people know, and it stays that way."

"It never leaves this room," I assured him.

Everything seemed settled.

Edward stood up and looked at his younger brother.

"I'm still worried, Jack."

"Don't worry. Everything'll be all right."

[Philip Whitson]

Chapter 13

Red Rock

Friday, May 22nd

I held up my Winchester.

I was all alone, mounted, waiting beside the tracks south of Red Rock. In the middle of nowhere. Within the wide Sonoran expanse of barren mesas and desert arroyos. Amid the scattered mesquite, creosote, and buckhorn.

When the engineer saw me, he slowed down his long train, bringing it to a gradual stop right beside me. Eventually, from the other side of the train, I heard a stock door open. Then I heard a ramp coming down, then the hooves of his black horse Night. Then the ramp went back up again, and the door closed.

Some kind of signal must have been given.

Slowly, the train started moving again.

Patiently, I waited for it to pass.

When it was finally gone, amid trails of dust, I could see Jack mounted on his black stallion, wearing his black Stetson, wearing his usual black clothes.

He directed Night across the tracks.

"Welcome home, Jack!" I said excitedly.

Jack smiled.

"How's my favorite Texan?"

"Just right."

He nodded.

"I hear you're doing a great job at Rising Sun," he said.

I was flattered into silence.

Then Jack took a moment to look around, staring at the endless Sonoran Desert.

"It's good to be back home."

Two days ago, he'd telegrammed from Prescott explaining that his luggage would be forwarded to Rising Sun from the station in Tucson. Which is why I was sent alone to meet him near Red Rock. Back at Rising Sun, Red Star was preparing a "welcome back" fandango for later tonight.

But I had a message.

"John says that everything's ready."

Jack was pleased and unsurprised, and I knew the message had nothing to do with a welcome home party.

"Jack," I said, "I know that you and John are up to something, and I'd like to be a part of it."

He thought it over.

"You know that I can handle a gun," I reminded him.

"Yes, but who'll run the herd? Don't we have about eight hundred head grazing the valley?"

"Yeah, but Suárez can do it. You can check with Red Star."

He looked at me intently.

"You sure you want this, Jim?"

He didn't bother to add, "Do you know it'll be dangerous?" because he knew that I already knew.

I nodded yes.

"All right, Jim. You'll be riding with Red Star."

"I'll be ready."

He nodded back, as if to say, "I know you will."

Then he looked to the west.

"Let's go home, Jim."

"We'll be celebrating tonight, Jack!"

He smiled.

He knew.

"Of course, we will."

Then we rode west together across the desert basin toward the Saucedas and Rising Sun.

[Jim Ellis]

Chapter 14

"Caminito"

Friday, May 22nd

I watched Jack from the dark periphery.

The party was underway.

Everyone was having fun.

The families, the adults, the kids.

Under the moonlight, amid the many soft lanterns.

I was unconsciously swaying softly to the *rancheras*, the ranch songs being played and sung, accompanied by two fiddles, an accordion, two Spanish guitars, and a mandolin. Many "Suners" (those of us who lived in the Rising Sun Valley) were dancing in the open area between the main house and the storage barn. Dancing quadrilles, waltzes, and occasional reels. But even more were simply talking, eating, and laughing. It seemed that everyone was enjoying Jack's welcome home party: Jack's Anglos, my Papagos, the Mexican ranch hands, Padre Luis, and the pretty Pima named White Dove.

Not too pretty, I hope.

Jack looked surprisingly refreshed after his long trip from the east and his stop in Prescott to see his older brother. He was dressed in fresh black clothes, without a hat, with his guns and a new black neckerchief. He was also wearing a black canvas jacket against the cool night air.

Yes, I was listening to the music, but I was also listening to my heart beat with a young girl's desires and infatuation. Watching as Jack was swarmed by all the Suners welcoming him back, as Red Star stood silently at his side. Eventually, Jack made his way to Running Brook. To pay his respects. The old man, the patriarch, stood up, and they embraced. Soon Padre Luis joined them, and John looked over at the musicians who brought their lively *ranchera* to a slightly rushed conclusion.

Everyone fell silent, turning to face Running Brook as he offered Jack an earthen cup. Probably wine. Maybe ceremonial wine. Maybe Port.

It was time for a toast.

John pulled over a chair, and Jack stood up on the seat and raised his cup.

Into the night.

"May the Lord protect us," he said simply. "And protect our valley."

That was it.

Just a few words, but the right words.

All the adults drank to his toast, everyone cheered, and even a few *gritos Mexicanos* were heard. Eventually, John nodded back at the musicians who began to play again.

It was probably time for me to do something.

In the nine months that Jack had been away, I knew exactly what had happened to me. To my body. To my mind. I was no longer a silly impulsive little tomboy. Yes, I was still at the corral with the horses every single day, but I'd also started to become a woman. I started to understand what my confusing feelings last year actually were.

What those confusing feelings actually meant.

I made my way toward him.

Into the crowd.

He sensed me and turned.

"*Bienvendido a casa*," I said.

Simply.

It was clear that he was glad to see me, but he also seemed unsure how he should react.

"It's good to be home, Moonlight."

He smiled his smile.

"You've grown up on me," he added.

I nodded, but I didn't blush in the least because I was expecting it. After all, my mother had a mirror in the house, and I knew I wasn't the same little fourteen-year-old he'd last seen last August.

I was wearing a beautiful traditional red dress, made by my mother, with Papago trims, with a beaded necklace, with a white desert hibiscus in my dark hair.

"Can I show you something?" I said.

"Of course."

"*Que te valla vien*," I said.

Unlike his Latin, Jack's Spanish was sometimes rather perfunctory, but he knew enough to follow me.

We walked away from his fandango toward the horse corral.

The moon and the party lamps spread a soft hazy light over about half of the seemingly empty corral.

We could still hear the music.

I opened the gate, whistled softly, and Midnight emerged from the darkness. He was now a brilliant black stallion. He kicked up a little bit, then came over to me obediently. Gently. He lowered his head, and I rubbed his crest.

"He's incredible," Jack said, clearly impressed.

"I told you he'd be a great one! I've taken very good care of him."

"I can see that."

"It was the best present that I've ever received."

Jack didn't know what to say, so I gently slapped my stallion's flank, and he ran off into the darkness again.

Jack remained silent, which was nothing new.

"I know you're riding out soon," I said.

I tried not to sound as worried as I was.

"This is to keep you safe," I said.

I placed my little gift into his hand. It was a small Francis Xavier medal and chain that had been crafted by my uncle from Sonoran silver.

He looked it over in the moonlight.

"St. Francis," he said. "It's beautiful."

Then he removed his black bandana, tucked it in his back pocket, and put the medal and chain over his head and around his neck.

"He'll bring me back to you," he said. "He'll bring *all* of us back."

Then we heard the band playing and singing the lovely *canción ranchera*, *"Caminito."*

"Isn't that one of your favorites?" he asked.

I was astonished that he remembered.

He looked down into my eyes, and he took my left hand into his own, which startled me at first. Then he placed his own left hand gently around to my back, and we danced.

Lightly, with very little movement.

In the silver moonlight.

Romantically.

Without a word.

As I wondered what was actually happening. If what I thought and hoped was happening was actually happening.

[Moonlight]

Chapter 15

Hacienda

Friday, May 22nd

Yeah, I felt out of place.

I didn't say a word.

Neither did anyone else.

We were sitting in Matthias's old wooden study, lit with lamps, amid the many bookshelves where Jack and John had once been educated.

Religious books, Bibles, Shakespeare, Virgil, Cicero, Aquinas, philosophers I'd never heard of, poets I'd never heard of, histories (lots of them), Dickens, Scott, Byron, Austen, Melville, etc.

All those volumes were as silent as those sitting around the room sipping Port. Yes, Port! Which was a taste picked up by Jack's father Matthias on a trip to Brazil many years ago when he met his second wife, Jack's mother.

We were sitting around a low wooden table covered with maps, sitting in a kind of circle, clearly waiting on Running Brook, the old

Papago, the Rising Sun patriarch. There were five of us besides the old medicine man, all of whom it seemed would be participating in whatever it was that Jack and John were planning.

The purpose that night was clearly to secure the old Indian's approval for whatever the plan was.

So you've asked me to describe, from my outsider's point of view, the six men in the room besides Jack.

Here goes:

Running Brook: Seventy-eight years old, Running Brook once rode with Matthias and Grey Wolf back in the olden times. Despite his many years, he's still Rising Sun's medic ("medicine man"), familiar with both modern medicines as well as traditional remedies. He's also the proud grandfather of Dark Sky.

John Red Star: The son of Yellow Dawn and Grey Wolf, the co-founder of Rising Sun Ranch. He's Jack's best friend. They're said to be "blood brothers," whatever that means. After the deaths of Matthias Shannon and Grey Wolf, Red Star and John took over the reins at Rising Sun. John is an experienced Papago warrior, who lost his parents to smallpox when he was thirteen years old. He grew up alongside Jack and was equally well-educated. He handles the finances at Rising Sun, oversees the reservoir and the grain mill, as well as the stables with Jack. Most important, he oversees security for the entire valley. He's the best man I've ever seen with a Winchester (he carries a Model 1873 lever-action), and he's also a master of traditional weaponry. I was once told that he could fire twenty arrows from horseback in less than a minute. I have no idea if that's even possible.

Coyote: A Papago warrior and legendary tracker, forty-two, highly-skilled. Especially adept with his double-barrel, specifically the 1878 Colt shotgun known as the "crowd tamer." He's essentially in charge of protection at Rising Sun. Every day he undertakes serious mortifications and self-discipline to make himself more potent and powerful. Once devoted to Grey Wolf, he's now completely devoted to Red Star and Jack.

Dark Sky: My age, around twenty-two, Dark Sky is a young Papago warrior, the grandson of Running Brook and the protégé of Coyote. He's cheerful, but watchful, always observant, always ready to do whatever is needed. A very close friend of Jack and John. And me.

Me: Born San Marcos, Texas, age twenty-four, hired at Rising Sun as a cattle drover by Red Star and Cody Clayton, my mentor, now deceased, whom I replaced as the ranch's cattle-driver. I might be sitting in a strange library with Jack and a bunch of silent Indians, but I've never felt more at home than living here at Rising Sun. I consider Dark Sky, Jack, and John my closest friends.

I hope that's helpful.

So I sat there like the rest of them and waited.

Eventually, Running Brook put down his cup of Port and looked over at Jack.

It was time.

Jack bowed his head in the old man's direction, then he stood up, looked down at the Rising Sun patriarch, and wasted no time.

"Red Star will ride southwest to Sasabe with Coyote, Dark Sky, and Jim, to meet with Padre Rillito. Then they'll continue over the border into Sonora."

He looked over at John.

"John," he explained, "has already contacted the Mexican author-ities."

John confirmed with a nod of his head.

Naturally, I had no idea what was going on, so Dark Sky slid an old map in front of me and traced the routes so I could follow along.

Jack continued.

"At the same time, I'll ride southwest to Elfrida, where Stark's been staying. When everything's finished, we'll all meet at the mission near Hanging Rock."

I looked at Dark Sky, who pointed at the map and whispered.

"San Xavier del Bac."

Which I'd heard of, which I could see marked on the map. "Then," Jack continued, "Coyote and Dark Sky will take the prisoners to Jack-son's ranch outside Prescott, and John, Jim, and I will go after Brady."

He admitted a potential difficulty.

"Which might take some time since Brady double-crossed and killed his old partners before he took to the mountains near Tucker Mines."

Jack finished.

"Then we'll go to Jackson's, and we'll all ride into Prescott. Once they're safely confined, everyone will return home to Rising Sun, except for John and me and Jim. We'll stay to the end."

The old Indian thought it over.

It seemed like an hour.

Finally, he spoke. I'd never actually heard him speak before, and he sounded exactly like he looked. Aged, confident, serious.

"I don't like you going to Elfrida alone."

Jack was prepared.

"John has mentioned the same thing, so I plan to elicit support from Douglass Tyler, the US Deputy Marshall in Elfrida."

The old man looks at him suspiciously.

"Is that a promise?"

Jack was forthright.

"Yes."

Which settled it.

The old Papago was satisfied.

"Then ride in the morning, young men. But remember that the best riders ride not with vengeance in their hearts but with justice."

Everyone agreed with their silence.

Including me.

[Jim Ellis]

Editor's Note

Tohono O'odham:

The Tohono O'odham tribe ("People of the Desert"), known more generally as the Papago, are pueblo Indians of the Sonora Desert who generally keep to themselves in their water-scarce environment. They tend to live in small villages, in neat clean adobe brick homes. They maintain livestock, but subsist mostly by farming, cleverly irrigating their fields with diverted mountain streams and catch basins for occasional flash floods. They grow corn, wheat, tepary beans, squash, Papago peas, and Spanish watermelons, and they also cull the fruit of the Saguaro cactus. They make porridges, stews, and drink coffee. They also ferment ceremonial wine, but they only drink alcoholic spirits on special occasions.

They have cordial relations with most of their neighbors, including the Pima, the Zuma, and the Maricopa. Like all those tribes, they live under the constant threat of the nomadic Apache (which means "enemy" in the Zuni language) from the north who subsist by raiding other tribes for food, livestock (especially horses), and, on occasion children, whom they raise as their own. This threat has existed in the Southwest for hundreds of years, and the Papago, in response, have developed within each of their small clusters a band of highly-trained warriors to protect their homes and livestock.

Having said that, the Tohono O'odham are essentially a peaceful people, who have, in general, maintained good relations with both the Spanish who migrated into the area in the late 1600s, as well as the American Anglos who mostly arrived after the Gadsden Purchase of 1854, mostly to graze cattle on the extensive Sonoran grasslands. In the past, the Papago have, on various occasions, joined with the whites in ventures against marauding Apaches. They've also wisely leveraged those past cooperations to successfully obtain federal land rights to sections of their traditional territories.

Although still devoted to traditional ways, most Papagos were Christianized by Spanish missionaries, particularly the Jesuit Eusebio Kino, who with the help of the Papago Indians built the original mission church at San Xavier del Bac in 1700.

Note: The word "Arizona" derives from a Tohono O'odham word meaning "small spring."

Chapter 16

South Ridge

Monday, May 25th

We were riding out of the valley.

Over South Ridge.

Soon Jack would be going his own way alone.

John stopped, and we all did the same.

Five of us.

Jack, Red Star, Coyote, Dark Sky, and me.

Red Star sat immobile in his saddle with his weapons visible and ready. His Winchester on his right. His traditional bow on his left. Then he stared back at Rising Sun down below us in the valley. Maybe it was something that he always did whenever he was leaving home for a while.

I looked down like everyone else, squinting a bit in the bright Arizona sun, seeing the main house hacienda, its fluttering American flag, the nearby white adobe homes, the red barns, the wooden stables, the corral, the white chapel with its high cross, and all the cattle lazily grazing off in the distance.

"Three weeks at the mission," Jack said.

John nodded.

"Be careful, Jack."

Then Coyote turned in his saddle, looked over at Red Star, and smiled.

Which was a rarity.

"John."

When John and the rest of us looked over, Coyote pointed back across the valley to a distant ridge, and I strained in the sunlight to see the distant figure of a young girl dressed in buckskins sitting on a fabulous black stallion. When Moonlight saw us looking, she took off her hat and waved across the valley. John and Coyote waved back. Jack tipped his hat.

"She's a woman now, Jack," John said.

With all that that implied.

"I know," Jack said.

Then he and all the rest of us rode off in silence.

[Jim Ellis]

Editor's Note

Matthias and Grey Wolf:

This account might include some amplifications, maybe even some mythology, and surely some omissions, but it is, however, the best that I can accurately summarize from multiple sources of varying reliability.

Matthias Padraig Shannon (Jack's father) was born in Louisiana Territory, in Missouri, in 1796. His Irish immigrant father was a farmer of multiple crops who also did some horse breeding. Matthias was the oldest of five children, the rest being female. In his youth, he worked hard with his father to support the family, as he developed a special interest in horse breeding.

At eighteen, he joined the US Army, served in the cavalry, participated in the Battle of New Orleans, then fought for several years against the Seminoles. Originally, he felt it was justified, given the Seminoles treatment of other tribes in the area, but in time he decided that things had gone too far.

In 1824, the key year in his life, at the age of twenty-eight, he left the army as a cavalry captain, and with his own savings and a small inheritance from a maternal Irish uncle, he traveled to Albuquerque where he purchased three stallions and nine well-bred mares. His intention was to sell them in Mexico to one of the wealthy *caballeros* and offer himself as a breeder.

He headed south into Arizona, alone with his twelve horses. He seemed unaware or maybe unconcerned about the constant Apache threat, especially given their well-known lust for quality horses. While traveling through a narrow pass in the Santa Rosa Mountains, he came upon a wounded Indian who'd been left for dead by the Apaches who'd stolen his horse. The Papago was unconscious, lying in the dirt, penetrated by an arrow in his left thigh and another in his left shoulder. He was clearly dying from blood loss, thirst, and exposure.

Matthias immediately tended to the dying man and somehow brought him back to life. Some accounts say this recuperation took two weeks, some say a month. Regardless, the dying man eventually regained consciousness as well as his health. His name was Grey Wolf. He was a Papago warrior who spoke proper English and had been waylaid by a band of Chiricahua Apaches.

During the time they spent together, the two men became close friends. They talked during those many long hours about, as they say, "everything under the sun." Including their dreams. Their aspirations. Matthias's dream of a breeding farm. Grey Wolf's dream of his own Papago ranch. When he was asked about the water scarcity problem, Grey Wolf told Shannon about an isolated valley which he called Rising Sun, where he wanted to create a reservoir to preserve the mountain waters of the Saucedas.

They decided to combine their dreams. Matthias knew livestock, and he had some money and horses. Grey Wolf was the leader of a small contingent of about forty Papagos, mostly warriors and farmers and their families.

They undertook an oath of some kind.

Or, as claimed by some, a pact in blood.

Then they went into the valley together, explored every inch, made extensive plans, and were convinced that that they could achieve what they desired to achieve.

Chapter 17

Topawa

Wednesday, May 27th

It's beautiful, but brutal.

We came through a pass in the Comobabi Mountains, then down to the floor of the desert. A stark world of saltbrush, bursage, mesquite, cholla cacti, and sun.

With more sun.

A blazing sun.

In a dry cracked moistureless world.

Then off in the distance we saw a thin column of smoke trailing into the white blue sky. John looked over at Coyote who had seen it as well.

We all had.

Coyote nodded, and we rode off at a faster clip.

Twenty minutes later, we came around a steep rocky escarpment and rode slowly and silently within the gruesome scene that lay before us. A family of whites, clearly Mormons, lay dead and blood-covered in the dirt. Massacred. A father, a woman, and two young children. Their little encampment of two canvas tents as well as their travel wagon had been burned to the ground. Their horses and other possessions were gone.

Coyote dismounted and looked around in the midst of the slaughter.

We all knew who'd done what had been done, but John said it anyway, in a whisper.

"Apache."

We waited a bit, until Red Star finally broke the silence, addressing Coyote.

"How many?"

"Four."

Dark Sky was unable to restrain himself.

"They've broken their own peace!"

I didn't even know there'd been another peace, since all those agreements came and went with such frequency.

John looked at Dark Sky.

"These are outcasts. They're renegades."

But no one was comforted by the fact.

Coyote looked up at John.

"They've taken someone with them. A young one. A child."

John thought it over.

We were on a schedule, with not much leeway, but like the rest of us, he wants to pursue.

He turned again to Coyote.

"How far?"

"We could catch them before sundown."

When John nodded, Coyote mounted with a quick leap, and instantly, we all rode out at high speed.

[Jim Ellis]

Chapter 18

Jennifer's First Letter

Wednesday, May 27th

My Dearest,

I hope you had a pleasant trip west, I hope you had a pleasant visit with your brother in Prescott, I hope you're happily back with your family and friends, and I hope that you've been thinking about me every minute of every day.

As I have you.

I know that I promised not to bombard you with letters, but it's been hard. When you were gone but a single hour, I began to feel the terrible weight of loneliness, and I hope to never again watch the railroads take away the one I love.

My life is very much the same, but I wish I was there with you in a part of the world I've never seen, which I try to comprehend as best I can. Instead, I've sent you a remembrance. A photograph of me taken at Menlo Park. I hope you like it.

I know you're not much of a letter writer, but you promised one every three weeks, so I've begun checking the post.

Be safe my love and write as you've promised. I wait for the summer to pass away and for you to come back to me again.

The one who loves you, Jennifer

Chapter 19

Topawa Basin

Wednesday, May 27th

We'd raced through a tight arroyo and cut them off at Topawa Basin, just as all four of them rode into a narrow grey-lit canyon. Apaches are brave and very smart. They're hit-and-run raiders who rely on stealth, subterfuge, and the unexpected, often ambush.

They're not used to being surprised themselves.

Well, we certainly surprised them.

The leader of their small band was a fierce-looking Apache warrior, about forty years old, who was mounted on a fabulous brown-and-white pinto.

Since you've asked me to describe him, I'll do my best.

Like most Apache warriors, he wore a white cotton tunic with puffy Spanish sleeves and loose cotton Mexican pants. He also wore an impressive leather vest with beaded designs, leather moccasins, and a wide red headband around his shoulder-length black hair. I was told later that the color red was a marker of his past prowess as both a warrior and a raider. He also had a stripe of white paint across his face, across the bridge of his nose, extending horizontally over his high sun-browned cheekbones.

He was, if truth be told, rather magnificent.

Intimidating.

His three Apache companions seemed no less fierce, looking very much the same but without the face paint, and wearing white head-bands, not red. Behind them trailed five horses and a packhorse, on which the child, dressed in riding clothes, was bound to the saddle's pommel and gagged through the mouth.

All four raiders had leather gunbelts, handguns, and, most impor-tantly, quality Winchesters.

They were approaching slowly and silently through the canyon pass. Unexpectedly, around a sharp bend, they came upon John Red Star, waiting on his horse, immobile, blocking their pathway. I noticed that John had now switched his weapons. His Winchester was now at his left, and his bow was now ready at his right.

The Apaches stopped where they were, as their leader stared coldly at Red Star, clearly sizing him up. I was off to the side thinking to myself that this was the same deadly confrontation that had been going on for hundreds of years.

Before Geronimo, before Cochise, before Victorio.

Before the Tonto Wars and all the other wars.

A kind of inter-tribal vendetta.

Immediately, the rest of us rode out beside Red Star to face the Apaches. Coyote and Dark Sky to his right, with me to his left.

No weapons had been drawn.

John spoke.

"Those are not your horses."

He spoke in the Apache dialect of a language known as Athapascan, but I knew what he was saying.

It was simple enough.

The Apache leader smiled and spoke in English with obvious condescension.

"The Papago speaks Apache."

John, unmoved, repeated himself.

"Those are not your horses."

"They're Apache now."

It was said with contempt, but, as far as he was concerned, it was the truth. One thing that's undeniable about the Apaches is that they never lie.

They detest liars.

As far as he was concerned, the horses may have once belonged to white Mormons, but now they were his.

Now they were Apache.

Dark Sky had had enough.

"You're renegades!" he said in English. "Apache outcasts!"

The insult infuriated the Apache leader. Immediately he bolted toward John, simultaneously pulling his rifle. At the same time, the other three Apaches, who remained in their places, also pull their rifles. We did the same. There was a violent exchange. As you know, Papagos have extraordinary expertise with the rapid-fire lever-action Winchester .44, and I'm not too bad myself.

Coyote, of course, preferred his Colt shotgun.

When it was over, all three Apaches were dead and fallen from their horses. Dark Sky had been struck in his left shoulder, but he was still mounted. Then I looked over and saw the Apache leader lying dead on the rocky ground with an arrow protruding from his neck. I wish I had seen how it had happened. Although it seemed improbably impossible, Red Star, while still mounted, arrowed his bow and killed the attacking Apache leader before the warrior's Winchester was fired.

Coyote dismounted, helped Dark Sky down to the ground, and examined his wound.

John waited.

"How is it?" he asked.

Dark Sky answered for himself.

"I'm fine."

Coyote ignored him.

"It's through. Not too bad."

Satisfied, I also dismounted, went over to the packhorse, and cut the cords at the pommel. Then I pulled the child from the horse, cut the other binds, and removed the gag. Then I lifted the hat and turned around to face Red Star.

Surprised.

"It a girl."

A pretty one, I thought to myself.

Almost broken, she said nothing. I bent down, lifted her head, and let her drink from my canteen.

She looked up into my eyes.

[Jim Ellis]

Chapter 20

Elfrida

Thursday, May 28th

I want to be clear about something.

It wasn't my choice.

My hands were tied.

Those bastards in Prescott wouldn't let me do a thing even though I was a US Marshal appointed by the President of the United States.

Fortunately, Stark hadn't caused any trouble since he'd arrived in town about a month ago, living at the Elfrida Hotel.

So we went our separate ways.

Until the kid showed up.

Who never told me his name.

I was sitting at my desk one Thursday afternoon in May 1885 when he walked into my office.

He was tall, lean, and armed. He was also young and handsome and trouble.

I looked up.

"What can I do?" I said.

He wasted no time.

"I've come for Stark, and I plan to take him back to Prescott for trial."

If any other kid had walked into my office and said something that stupid, I would have laughed in his face and told him to get the hell out of my town.

But this kid was no laughing matter.

"He'll kill you," I said, as a matter of fact.

He ignored me, stepped forward, and placed some official documents on the desk in front of me. I looked them over carefully.

Needless to say, I was impressed.

I looked up at the kid again.

"The Attorney General signed these," I said.

It wasn't really a question.

I felt I should explain myself.

"I've been ordered to leave Stark alone."

"Why?"

"I don't know," I admitted.

"Maybe they're afraid of losing one of their best."

It was a nice thing for him to say, and I appreciated it. Sure it's true that I probably wasn't as adept as Damien Stark, but I still wasn't afraid of him. I'd been dealing with his kind for over twenty years.

Regardless, the kid seemed unconcerned that he was on his own.

"I'll take care of Stark, but I'll need some help getting him out of town. You'll need a buckboard and a driver."

I stood up.

"Fine."

"Where's the doctor's office?" he asked.

"Down near the saloon."

Then just before he left my office, he asked me an odd question.

"Is Stark right-handed or left?"

"Right. Does it make any difference?"

"Not much," he said rather off-handedly, then he left and stepped out into the street.

Eventually, he headed down to the Elfrida Saloon. Since I was off getting the buckboard, I wasn't there, but the local boys told me all about it afterwards.

Elfrida Tavern's a refuge for everyone in town, as well as a hold-out for all kinds of sketchy characters, including a handful of criminal types. On that particular afternoon, the place was noisy and active. Someone was playing the upright, men were drinking and playing cards, and the women were selling themselves as usual. Stark, quietly and unobtrusively, was drinking at the center of the bar, talking with one of the regular bargirls. He wore, as he always did, a neat white shirt, a black vest, and a Colt .45.

Then old doc Watson came into the bar and went up to Stark. He was carrying his medical bag, and he seemed a bit confused.

As if uncertain how to proceed.

Stark looked at him coolly but not belligerently.

"Well?"

The doc responded awkwardly.

"I was told that you'd be needing me."

Stark was amused.

"Who told you that?"

"A young man dressed in black, with a black bandana covering most of his face."

Stark immediately realized what was happening, and he seemed delighted.

"Did he give a name?"

"Yes. Retribution."

"It's about time," Stark said softly, as if to himself.

"He also told me to give you this."

The old man held out a small folded note.

Stark smiled.

"Read it."

But the doc was uneasy.

"He said it was for afterwards."

Stark smiled again.

He was enjoying the game.

He took the note and finished his drink.

"Where is he?"

"Out in the street."

Stark left the saloon.

When he saw the kid waiting, he seemed more than pleased.

As already described, the kid had a black bandana pulled up to his eyes, even though it was a bright still day with no wind and little dust. Beneath his Stetson and above his bandana, all that could be seen of his face were his dark intense eyes.

Stark, still holding the note in his hand, calmly walked to the center of the now-deserted street, staring hard at the kid. Then he tucked the note into his left shirt pocket and moved closer.

"I've been waiting for you," he said.

There was no response, which had no effect on the supremely confident Damien Stark.

He was enjoying himself.

"I'll soon be looking down at the face you're hiding."

Again, there was no response.

Stark got serious.

"When you killed the Reicher brothers in Gayleyville, you killed my best friends."

This time there was a single-word response from beneath the black bandana.

"Good."

It was clear that nothing else needed to be said, as the two men waited on each other in the white-sun silence beneath a cloudless Arizona sky.

Suddenly, Stark made his move, and the kid responded.

Two shots were fired.

The first bullet hit Stark above his gun hand at the wrist, and his Colt flew away into the street. The second struck him in the left thigh. He immediately grasped at it, then slumped down to the street.

Stark had never fired his weapon.

Not once.

Slowly, the kid holstered his Colt and whistled for his horse, as more and more people, stunned by what they'd seen through the windows of the saloon and the other storefronts, gradually exited onto the street.

I immediately pulled up with the buckboard, George Watson, and Stark's horse from the town stables. The kid's horse was already waiting at the center of the street, as the kid stood silent above the wounded and bleeding Stark.

As I stopped the buckboard beside them, the doctor rushed out of the saloon and over to Stark.

Since the crowd began to edge closer, I gave them a warning.

"Everyone will be wise to stay back."

Which they did.

Then the kid mounted his black stallion and looked down at Stark again.

The doctor turned and looked up at the kid.

"He'll be all right, but he'll never use that hand again."

Despite the implications of what the doctor had said, despite his obvious pain, Stark was unbowed.

He looked up at the kid.

"You're fast, kid, but you can't shoot straight."

The kid sat motionless on his horse. Then he gently tapped his chest with his right hand, and Stark remembered the note. Like me and everyone else, Stark was curious. With his good hand, he removed the note from his shirt pocket and handed it to the doctor.

The doc read it, seemingly amazed.

We all waited.

Finally, the doctor read it out loud.

Four words with a comma.

"Right wrist, left thigh."

I must say, I was a bit awestruck.

Then the kid turned his horse and rode slowly up the street to wait at the edge of town.

In the meantime, the doctor quickly bound the gunman's leg and bandaged his wrist. Then George and I immediately loaded Stark into the buckboard.

I looked back at the crowd.

"I expect *no* trouble."

They knew that I meant it, and no one seemed inclined otherwise.

Then George and I rode the wagon after the kid.

Whom I never ever saw again after that day in Elfrida.

Maybe he knew that I'd never see him again, and that was why he'd let me see his face when he came into my office.

Or maybe it was because he trusted me. Trusting that I would never describe him to anyone else. That I would understand that he wanted to remain anonymous for some reason, and that I'd be fine with whatever his reasons might be.

So I never knew who he was until today.

Until you showed up.

For which I'm grateful.

[US Marshal Douglas Tyler, retired]

Chapter 21

Sasabe

Friday, May 29th

He was standing in the cemetery.

Close to the blackened ruins of the destroyed church, once known as *Capilla del Espiritu Santo*, in Sasabe, Arizona, a tiny border town in Altar Valley.

The padre was a thin man, maybe sixty or so, with an expressive face.

It was clear why he wanted to meet us here. He wanted us to see the graves.

He pointed.

"We buried them here," he said.

Twenty-eight people, including twelve children, had died in the explosion six months ago.

There were fresh flowers on many of the graves.

At first, nothing more was said.

We sat on our horses and waited.

John, Coyote, Jim, and me.

They wanted to leave me in town with the horses and the Mormon girl, but I convinced them that I was fine. My arm was bandaged, and even if I couldn't handle a rifle as well as usual, I could still use a handgun, so John relented.

Eventually Juan Rillito, the Franciscan in a brown robe with a wooden cross at his chest, blessed himself and looked up at Red Star.

"John Red Star?"

"Yes."

They continued in Spanish.

"Even after six months, the town is still devastated."

"When did you arrive?"

"I was sent down from Tucson a week later."

"You have bruises on your face. Have you been beaten?"

He was forthright.

"Yes, three days ago."

"Why didn't they kill you?" John wondered.

"I'm not sure. I guess they believe that they have nothing to fear. The nearest law is up in Tucson, and they seem to be protected up there. They walk around this town like they own it."

"Where's Rodriquez now?"

"He's living in the home of the mayor he killed. A man named Ethan Cortez. He also killed his wife and his two little daughters."

It was hard to fathom.

"How many are there?"

"Just three, counting Rodriquez. There's also a woman."

"Is she there willingly?"

"I don't think so. When I asked about her the other day, they beat me in the middle of town."

"Has your man arrived from Tucson?"

"Yes."

John seemed satisfied.

It was time to do something.

Two hours later, in the middle of the hot afternoon, Luis Rodriquez and his two Mexican *compañeros* were eating outdoors at a large wooden table set in front of the Mayor's white wooden house. Beneath the shade of two high cottonwoods. They wore holstered guns and crossed cartridge belts in the Mexican fashion. Despite their long history of violence and barbarity, they ate mostly in silence, waited on by a pretty señorita. It was surprisingly pleasant and civilized. When Rodriquez finished his glass of wine, he called out for more.

"Violetta!"

She immediately refilled his glass.

The men seemed to be enjoying themselves.

They never heard us coming.

Coyote came around the back of the house with his double-barrel and stared directly at all three men.

Rodriquez immediately grabbed his Winchester and stood up.

His companions did the same.

Then Jim and I came up to Coyote with our own weapons. Ready but unaimed. Rodriquez was confident, but cautious. Not overly alarmed. Then John rode around the side of the house on his great appaloosa.

Rodriquez was dismissive.

"Run along, Papagos."

John ignored his insult.

Rodriquez just smiled and repeated himself.

"Run along, Indian scum."

The other two Mexicans, not so confident, lifted their rifles, and the subsequent exchange was fast and quick. As planned, Jim shot Rodriquez in the thigh, and Coyote and I fired at the other two. It happened so fast that Red Star didn't even bother to engage.

All three men were blown back to the ground from the table. One was dead from Coyote's double-barrel, one was struck in the stomach, and Rodriquez was clutching at his damaged thigh. Then, before we could react, the young woman Violetta stepped over to gut-shot *bandido* and slit his throat. When she turned on Rodriquez, Jim held her back and told her to go inside the house.

Which she did.

Wasting no time, Coyote immediately bound Rodriquez's hands behind his back, then tied the end of a long rope around his ankles. Then he tossed the other end of the rope over a sturdy branch on one of the cottonwoods, as he and Jim hoisted the man, upside down, off the ground.

I would say that his head was about two feet off the ground.

As this was going on, I noticed a small carriage approaching from the distance. So far, except for Violetta's unanticipated revenge, everything was going according to plan.

Rodriquez's bravado was completely bely gone.

"What do you want?" he called out to John who sat immobile on his horse.

No response.

Eventually, the carriage arrived and Padre Rillito walked over to the cottonwood trees. His companion, another older man who was wearing a city suit, went over to the table with his leather satchel and cleared off an area to do his work.

Rodriquez, dangling from his helpless position, looked up at the priest. It was clear that John's persistent refusal to speak had finally unnerved him.

"What do they want!"

"They want a signed confession, and they want the name of the man who hired you to destroy *Capilla del Espiritu Santo*."

It was perfectly clear that Rodriquez had done what he'd done because he'd been hired by one of the wealthy *caballeros* across the border. Father Rillito had his suspicions, but John wanted everything to be legal and well-documented. It was also believed that Rodriquez had similarly blown up a courthouse two years ago near El Puerto in Mexico.

For the same reasons.

"Fine," Rodriquez decided, "I'll confess to the church and take my chances in the Tucson courthouse, but I'll never mention any names but my own."

Even in his completely helpless position, Rodriquez felt somehow protected. Whoever had hired him clearly had political clout in Tucson.

The priest gave him another chance.

"These men want the name."

The upside-down pistolero was adamant.

"Just cut me down, and I'll sign whatever you want! But no names! Never!"

Disappointed, the priest walked away.

Then Coyote stepped forward. He was carrying a leather bag that he'd retrieved from the small carriage. He was also holding a "guiding" stick.

Without a word, he opened the bag and deposited the contents on the ground beneath the dangling head of Luis Rodriquez.

Personally, I don't care for those things, and Texas Jim likes them even less than me, but Coyote was fearless. I'd seen him wrangle those things more than once.

As for me, I preferred to shoot their heads off.

The snake fell into a pile of itself just below Rodriquez's face.

I suppose it was happy to be out of its bag, but it wasn't happy about much of anything else.

Its rattler rattled.

It was a dull brown diamondback. What they call a Western diamondback since I guess they have some similar version back east. But our diamondbacks are killers. They bite and kill more people than any other snake in Arizona, and they're huge. Some can grow longer than a man is tall. This one, I'd estimate, since it was wound around itself, was about forty-five-inches long.

As I mentioned, its black-and-white striped tail was now rattling, and even I was spooked a bit, and I was standing upright about ten feet away.

Needless to say, Rodriquez was panicked and terrified.

Who wouldn't be?

He begged in a whisper.

"Kill it!"

Coyote ignored him, then he took his stick and lightly tapped the ugly thing on the top of its head.

That did it.

"Cartas! It was Cartas! Domingo Cartas!"

The priest made sure.

"You'll sign to that effect?"

"Yes! Yes!"

Then Coyote adeptly wrangled the venomous thing back into its leather bag, just in case Rodriquez tried to go back on his word.

We cut the man down, took him to the table, and he signed all the legal documents with the leather snake bag sitting nearby on top of the table.

Still moving a bit from within.

[Dark Sky]

Chapter 22

Los Tajitos, Mexico

Monday, June 6th

H e was sleeping in the darkness.

We stood around his bed in the faint moonlight.

Red Star, Coyote, and me.

Dark Sky was waiting outside the hacienda.

All was quiet.

John struck a match, and his torch flamed over the bed. Immediately, Coyote grabbed the man by his hair and pulled him upright in his bed. Before Cartas realized what was happening, Coyote gagged him. Tightly. As I pressed the end of the barrel of my Winchester against his forehead, there was no resistance.

None.

An hour later, at the top of Sierra de los Tajitos, high above the valley, the wealthy border rancher Domingo Cartas, a bit overweight, about fifty, with dark thinning hair and a black moustache was directed to a small chair that was set about five feet from the edge of the cliff.

Cartas, blindfolded and gagged, was now wearing a dark overcoat in the cool night, draped over his sleeping clothes.

Coyote quickly bound him to the chair, then took off his gag and his blindfold. When his eyes adjusted, he looked down over the precipice and was terrified. When he attempted to speak, Coyote struck him a sharp blow in the face with the back of his hand. It was a warning blow, and Cartas got the message, and he sat quietly in his chair.

Terrified.

Red Star stepped forward, without expression as usual, and pulled out his knife, which glistened in the moonlight in front of Cartas's face. Then he placed the blade against the frightened rancher's cheek,

It was another warning.

When it was removed, it took Cartas a few moments to regain a bit of composure.

Finally, he spoke in Spanish.

"What do you want? I'm a rich man. I can pay you whatever you want."

"We'll get to that," John assured him.

Despite his circumstances, Cartas seemed somewhat relieved. As he waited in the silence, John slowly moved behind the rancher and his chair.

"How much did you pay Rodriquez to destroy the church in Sasabe?"

When Cartas hesitated, John put his foot against the back of the chair and gave it a shove toward the edge of the cliff.

It slid about three feet.

"Don't!" the man cried out in the night. "Please! Don't!"

Breathing hard, he blurted out an answer.

"I paid him $200 in gold, along with anything he wanted in Sasabe."

John moved to the man's side.

"Why?"

Cartas seemed uncertain what John meant.

John didn't hesitate.

He reached down, grabbed the chair, and slid it again.

A foot from the edge.

Cartas was horrified.

John repeated his question.

"Why did you have him do it?"

"Because I wanted more grazing land for my cattle."

Suddenly, the old priest appeared from the darkness, and he pulled Cartas's chair around to face him.

Cartas was naturally surprised but a bit relieved.

"Padre Rillito?"

The padre wasted no time.

"Do you swear it's the truth?"

"Yes. It's the truth! I swear it!"

"Did you also have Rodriquez destroy the courthouse in El Puerto?"

"Yes."

"What did you pay him for that?"

"A hundred dollars in silver."

"Why?"

"For the same reason. Land rights."

Satisfied, Father Rillito backed away, and Coyote cut off the rancher's bindings. Cartas, greatly relieved, stood up and took a cautionary step away from the edge of the cliff. Then from behind us in the darkness, we could hear the sound of Mexican spurs. Many. Many footsteps, many spurs. Eventually, in the torchlight, a uniformed Mexican Army Colonel appeared, accompanied by eight fully-armed soldiers.

Cartas, in shock, realized that he was finished. He stood in silence as the soldiers manacled his hands behind his back.

The colonel approached and looked at John.

"Red Star?"

"Your excellence," John nodded.

"Well done, young man, we now have fourteen witnesses."

But John had something else on his mind.

"Will he hang?" he asked.

The colonel looked coldly at Cartas.

"I have no doubt."

Satisfied, John looked over at the priest.

"Has everyone been cleared from the ranch?"

"Yes."

He looked at Dark Sky.

"Is everything else ready?"

"Yes."

As everyone looked out over the valley, Dark Sky handed John his long Papago bow with a single prepared arrow.

John looked at Cartas.

"How many years and how many murders did it take to build your empire?"

Cartas, as if in a trance, responded weakly.

"Many . . . many."

All was silent.

Tranquil.

John touched the tip of his arrow into Dark Sky's torch, then immediately fired a brilliantly flaming arrow that sailed upwards then over the valley, forming a fantastic flaming arch in the night sky. Until it finally struck the roof of the Mexican's hacienda. Instantly, the kerosene-soaked roof ignited, and with an extraordinary flash, the main ranch house exploded into flames. Then, in succession, just as we'd prepared, the barn, the bunk-house, and all the adjacent buildings flamed as well.

It was oddly beautiful, as everything conflated into an incredible blaze of light and sound and flame that filled the cool dark valley.

[Jim Ellis]

Chapter 23

San Xavier del Bal

Monday, June 15th

When I saw Night tethered outside the church, it was one of the best moments of my entire life. I'm sure that might seem rather strange, but dealing with Rodriquez was one thing, dealing with Damien Stark was another.

When we arrived at the entrance, Coyote and the others, along with Rodriquez and the Mormon girl, headed to the stables so they could rest the horses.

I dismounted.

It's fair to say that I take a special pride and gratification in the old mission. The previous church at San Xavier del Bal had been built by Padre Kino and my Tohono O'odham ancestors in 1692, but it was destroyed eight years later by raiding Apaches. The present and very beautiful church, also built by Tohono O'odham, was completed on the banks of the Santa Cruz in 1797.

Marvelously impressive.

White adobe, elaborate Spanish baroque.

Known as the "White Dove of the Desert."

I entered through its huge mesquite doorways into the interior of the church, amid the paintings, statues, religious carvings, and colorful frescoes.

Jack was sitting in the fourth row of the empty church, beneath a mural of the Pentecost, facing the altar.

All was silent.

I sat beside him and thanked God in my heart.

"Is everyone all right?" he asked.

"Yes. Dark Sky took a hit through his arm, but he's fine."

Jack nodded.

"How's Stark?" I asked.

"He's got a hole in his thigh."

I didn't think it appropriate to laugh in church, so I didn't.

"Which one?"

"Left."

I smiled.

Just as we'd planned.

Then it was Jack's turn.

"How's Rodriquez?"

"He's also got a hole in his thigh."

"Which one?"

"Guess."

Since he knew it wasn't necessary, we sat in the silence for a while.

In comfort.

Then Jack nodded over at the votive lights.

"I lit a candle," he said.

"For what?"

"That you'd come through that door."

[John Red Star]

Chapter 24

Hanging Rock

Monday, June 15th

After resting a bit at the mission, we headed across the hot-ter-than-hell desert plains into the Sierritas near Hanging Rock.

Where we set up camp for the night with two separate campfires.

Around midnight, I was sitting alone with Jack at the smaller fire. As I prodded the flames mindlessly with a wooden stick, Jack was resting comfortably against his Texas saddle.

Finally, I sat back with a cup of coffee.

As usual, Jack hadn't said much. Which is not to say that he was unfriendly in any way, it's just the way he always is. I remember my old man back in San Marcos, Texas, once saying, "Don't say nothin', Jim, unless someone asks you somethin'," which I never really practiced, being a bit of a talker myself, but maybe Matthias Shannon had once said something like that to his boy Jack, and it stuck.

Anyway, I couldn't keep my mouth shut.

"You know, Jack, there's one thing I never did understand about Red Star. Why did his father send him to live with the Apaches?"

"Well, Jim, there was a peace back then, and I think that Grey Wolf felt that John could learn a lot from his old enemies. Which he did."

"How old was he?"

"Twelve."

"It's still hard to figure."

Jack nodded.

"For us, it is."

Something else was bothering me.

"I heard that he rode with them as a boy. More than once."

"He did, but only after rustlers and renegades."

Which was quite a relief. I've always admired Red Star, and I was glad that Jack had cleared up my confusions.

Nevertheless, I *still* couldn't keep my mouth shut.

"I hope I'll do all right with Brady."

"You'll do just fine, Jim. Just as you did in Sasabe and Los Tajitos."

Which meant that John had told him that I'd done my bit, which I much appreciated.

Eventually, in the ensuing silence, John emerged from the outer darkness holding his Winchester. As always, his demeanor was imperturbable, but tonight his silent calm seemed less a matter of self-control and more a matter of relief, even relaxation.

Without a word, he sat across the fire from Jack, who smiled.

"How are our guests?"

"Coyote keeps them good company. Dark Sky too."

Jack was pleased.

He looked into the fire.

"We haven't had time to talk."

I didn't know exactly what that meant, but it sounded private, so I made a move to get up.

"I'll head over to Coyote," I said.

"No need," Jack said.

I looked over at Red Star who nodded agreement.

I must say, I was flattered and grateful, so I sat back again and just listened.

It seemed to me that John believed that the worst was over, and it was clear that they both felt perfectly content to be back in in each other's company. In my youth in Texas, I'd had my fair share of friends. The same at Rising Sun. Especially Dark Sky. But it was still hard not to be a bit envious of Jack and Red Star. They'd grown up together, except for John's year with the Apaches, and they seemed more like brothers than best friends. Actually, they seemed like both at the same time.

As for me, it seemed like a privilege to sit with them and listen.

Jack smiled.

"I heard you did it with an arrow."

Which clearly referred to John's killing the Apache warrior.

John just nodded.

Jack shook his head in disbelief, as did I.

Jack continued.

"What was that white girl doing on the Sasabe desert?"

"She was with her family."

"What were they doing there?"

"Mormons," John said.

As if that explained everything.

It was no secret that some Mormon families had begun moving south into Arizona.

"Proselytizing?" Jack asked rhetorically.

John shrugged.

"How old?"

"Seventeen."

I suddenly realized that Jack was teasing his best friend.

"A pretty girl?"

"Yes," John responded.

Matter-of-factly.

"I hear you've been rather solicitous."

John just shook his head, but Jack wasn't finished.

"Did you tell her that Tohono O'odham were Catholic a hundred and fifty years before Mormons existed?"

John smiled.

"Not yet."

Then John caught me smiling as well, so he brought me into it.

"Not as solicitous, I might add," he said to Jack, "as Mr. James Ellis is to the pretty Pima woman."

I stood my ground and responded honestly.

"You'll get no denials about that!"

Everyone at Rising Sun knew about my affection for White Dove and her little child, who Running Brook had cured of a fever ten months ago. When the child was brought back to health, John invited White Dove to stay in the valley, which she did.

Thank goodness.

Now that Jack had had his fun, John decided to turn the tables.

He looked across the lessening fire.

"What about Rutgers, Jack? I haven't heard very much."

Jack shrugged.

"I made some friends and saw some things," he said rather evasive-ly.

"Like what?"

"Like Menlo Park."

I was stunned.

"So what did he say?" John asked.

Yeah, I was aware that Jack had intended to talk to some Eastern engineers about our pumps, our viaducts, and our reservoir. And that he'd gone east with sketches, maps, and questions.

"He liked all of your improvements."

"Any suggestions?"

"A couple. Mostly topographical and equipment-related. Nothing serious. He seemed quite impressed."

I couldn't resist.

"You mean you actually talked to Thomas Edison?"

"I did, Jim. He's only ten miles from Rutgers, and he was very cordial."

I shut up.

Amazed.

To Jack, it seemed like nothing. Why shouldn't one man help another man with something? Even if one of the men was one of the most famous men in the entire world.

John wasn't finished.

He had his suspicions.

"You going back?"

"I'm not sure."

John waited for more, patiently.

As if "time" was a construct that never concerned him.

"Well, I do know one thing, John, I've got *no* interest in the law."

"I'm not surprised."

"Besides, I like it back here."

Which I guess meant that he wasn't planning to go back to Rutgers in the fall. Red Star seemed perfectly comfortable with the possibility, but he did raise another question.

"Then what about the girl?"

Yes, we all knew that Jack had a girlfriend back east. A young woman named Jennifer, but we didn't know how serious it was. We also knew that many years ago, Jack's father had gone east to St. Louis and come home with a bride, and that many years after that, after a visit to Brazil, he'd come back home again with his second wife, Jack's mother.

It now seemed that Jack's best friend had no idea just how serious Jack was about Jennifer.

Maybe Jack didn't know either.

"I don't know," he said simply.

There was another silence, then John reassured him.

"There's plenty of time, Jack"

"Right. Once we get this over with."

John seemed a little surprised.

"The worst is already done, Jack."

But Jack was cautious.

"Richard Brady's a dangerous man."

"Yes, but that's all he is."

[Jim Ellis]

Editor's Note

Rising Sun:

(As best I can put it together.)

Having agreed to their agreement, having secured a Mexican land grant for the entire valley, Matthias Shannon, Grey Wolf, and thirty Papagos built a huge stone damn in the Sauceda Mountains in 1835, located inside the Sauceda Wash below Moivavi. Which created the reservoir which they needed to irrigate their crops. This was also reinforced by a series of pumps to access underground water, which was more plentiful than one might have expected beneath the Sonoran Desert.

The following year, Matthias purchased a hundred head of longhorns in El Paso, Texas, and he and his mostly Mexican cattle hands drove them back to Rising Sun. Soon afterwards, he purchased six more quality colts and twenty-two brood mares in Las Cruces, New Mexico, to supplement his horse breedings at Rising Sun. In time, the main house was carefully constructed, being a two-part structure with Matthias in the north wing and Grey Wolf and Running Brook in the south wing. At the same time, many other adobe houses were built at the compound, as well as new barns, stables, and corrals. In 1830, the handsome white adobe chapel was built for Padre Luis, who'd been previously conducting Masses in one of the new barns.

When the Mexican War started in 1846, Rising Sun, still a part of Pimería Alta remained as neutral as possible. When the war concluded two years later, Arizona became the western half of New Mexico Territory. In 1850, Grey Wolf wisely initiated a treaty with the Apache, who never entered the valley again. Then, as a result of the Gadsden Purchase in 1854, the New Mexico Territory was expanded southward to include a large section of southern Arizona, which included Rising Sun.

On a more personal level, in 1851, at the age of fifty-five, Matthias met Kathleen Handcock on a business trip to St. Louis, and they married the following year at Rising Sun. Edward Shannon was born the year after that.

When the Civil War broke out in the east (1861), Rising Sun, although sympathetic to the North, again remained neutral in a territory of divided loyalties. In the same year, Kathleen Shannon, tragically died from a rattlesnake bite, and young Edward was sent to boarding school in St. Louis for his education, returning to Rising Sun every summer.

In 1863, Matthias, now a widower of sixty-seven, traveled on horse-related business to Rio de Janeiro, where he met Maria Barcelos, an elegant widow and the daughter of a wealthy Portuguese landowner and his Irish wife. Matthias and Maria married later that same year at Rising Sun, which was the same year that Arizona became its own territory, separated from New Mexico. The following year, Grey Wolf married a young Papago widow, Yellow Dawn.

In 1865, three months after the Civil War ended, Jack Shannon was born on July 4th. Ten days later (July 14th), John Red Star was born to Yellow Dawn and Grey Wolf, and the boys were raised together in the hacienda and on the ranch, strictly tutored by an elderly Rutgers classicist, Mr. Ezra Davenport.

During those years, the ranch prospered and became self-sufficient. Some of the ever-increasing cattle herd was sold to various Tohono O'odham settlements in the border regions, and others were driven to the stockyards in Albuquerque each spring. In time, other men with more resources began to create similar, often much larger, cattle ranches in southern Arizona, where their cattle could graze in the grasslands, in the meadows of sacaton and salt grass.

Henry Hooker founded his Sierra Bonita Ranch in 1872, and Walter L. Vail established Empire Ranch in Cienega Valley around the same time. Even Texas John Slaughter, a friend of John Chisholm, purchased the San Bernardino Ranch in Charleston, Arizona, in 1884. None of these huge enterprises, however, had any effect on Rising Sun, which kept to itself, worked hard, and created a good and comfortable place to live and thrive.

Nevertheless, even at Rising Sun, death lurked.

In 1873, Jack's mother Maria died of consumption when Jack was eight years old. Two years later, Matthias, age seventy-nine, fell from his horse on a narrow mountain trail and died from his injuries. Three years after that, smallpox crept into the valley and seven succumbed, including both Grey Wolf and Yellow Dawn. Red Star was thirteen years old.

In the aftermath, the Papago elder and medicine man Running Brook oversaw the valley in trust for the two teenaged sons. Finally, on July 14th, 1883, on Red Star's eighteenth birthday, Jack Shannon and John Red Star were officially invested as co-proprietors of Rising Sun Valley and the Rising Sun Ranch.

Chapter 25

Jennifer's Second Letter

Sunday, June 21st

My dearest Jack,

It's a lovely Sunday today, after church, sitting on my front porch, seemingly serene, yet torn up inside. Are you all right?

Have you forgotten me?

I have no way of understanding why you haven't written, so I do nothing but worry for you and for us. Despite my best efforts, I've become worthless to my students and my family.

To be honest, I had no idea that I was capable of such worry and fear, and no understanding, until now, of the depth of my feelings for you. Each passing day, both without you and without any acknowledgement grows more and more unbearable. So I continue to watch the mails, pray, and wait for something (anything) from my love.

Strangely enough, even though I've always been considered a strong and highly practical woman, I find myself unable to be ashamed of myself and of my feelings. I've always felt that we were nothing but totally honest with each other, so I'm being honest with you.

Please reassure the love that waits for you alone.

With love, with devotion, Jennifer

Chapter 26

Tucker Mining Company

Monday, June 29th

Silver.

The Tucker Mining Company.

It looked like quite an operation.

I'd never seen one before.

The four of us rode into Tucker, a small mountain mining town north of Globe, northwest of Phoenix, which is set rather precariously into the sides of the Aubrey Cliffs. All of the town's dark gray buildings as well as its other structures seemed to blend into the dark rocks of the mountainside.

Everything around us seemed an intractable maze of sheds, rail cars, quarries, tunnels, shafts, sluices, picks and hammers, and a hoard of relentless soot-covered workers drenched with sweat. As we rode along, I reminded myself to never again feel sorry for myself when I was out riding with the herd, even in storms, even in thunderstorms.

Eventually, we found the boss's small office cabin, and I followed Jack and Red Star inside, while Coyote waited outside with the horses.

A friendly kid was working a desk in the front room of the little two-room cabin.

He looked up at Jack.

"Can I help you, sir?"

Jack placed a few official documents on the desk in front of the young kid.

"We'd like to see whoever's in charge."

The boy quickly looked over the documents, then he immediately stood up and stepped over to the inner office doorway, addressing his boss.

"Mr. Driscoll, there's some strangers here to see you with documents from Prescott."

When Driscoll entered the room, he shook hands with Jack and John.

I stayed in the background.

From everything we'd heard about Stephen Driscoll, who managed the entire mining operation, he was efficient, fair, and hard-working. Somewhere in his fifties, Driscoll was once a miner himself, and he has no time for laziness, yet he was kind to his miners.

Everything we'd heard about him seemed to be true.

He glanced down at the documents, as Jack placed the Brady wanted poster in front of him on the desk.

"This is what we're looking for."

Driscoll looked at it and called over to the kid.

"Get Franklin in here."

As the kid ran off, Driscoll finished examining the documents and the poster.

He looked up at Jack.

Astonished.

"Six banks and nine murders?"

"Yes," Jack assured him.

"Well, I've never seen him, but maybe my foreman knows better."

We waited.

"How's the silver?" Jack asked.

"Not a bad year, but it's real rough work. I did it myself for fourteen years."

"It's the kind of hard work that can turn a territory into a state."

Driscoll clearly appreciated Jack's compliment, and he nodded in agreement.

Then Franklin, a hard and wiry man about forty years old, entered the office. He was filthy but pleasant.

Driscoll showed him the poster.

"Have you seen this man, Tom?"

Franklin took a look at the sketch.

"Sure, that's that crooked gambler that those two idiots Rawlins and McCoy ran off with. Get-rich schemes or something like that. I had no idea that he was a bank robber."

He was clearly disgusted.

"When did they leave?" Jack asked.

"About five days ago."

"Any idea where they were heading?"

"I heard something about a mountain cabin somewhere north of here."

Jack had heard all he needed to know. He collected his papers and tucked them beneath his vest.

But Driscoll asked for a favor.

"Those two miners really aren't such bad sorts. Maybe you can drop a load of sense on them."

"We definitely will," Jack assured the man. "We'll encourage them to get back here to Tucker."

Then Jack thanked both of the men, and we left.

It took us a week to find the mountain cabin.

In the darkness, Coyote and I came up behind McCoy, who was sitting watch above a mountain trail and smoking a cigarette. Up the path, there was a small wooden cabin with a large chimney resting against the mountain in an isolated canyon. Silently, Coyote came up behind the man and smashed the back of his head with the butt of his shotgun. When McCoy slumped to the ground unconscious, we quickly bound him, gagged him, and dragged him up to the cabin.

Twenty minutes later, after I'd helped Coyote and John do what they wanted to do with the man's unconscious body, I stationed myself, as instructed, just outside one of the small windows on the cabin's south side. Inside, the place was fairly well-lit with three lamps, and I could see Rawlins, the other young miner, sitting at a table and thinking about something that Brady had just told him. Richard Brady, tall and intimidating, hovered over the young man, standing close, with one foot up on a chair. He spoke firmly and authoritatively, and I could hear him clearly.

He was making an attempt to try and appear reasonable.

"That's the way it is, kid. If someone gets in the way, you've got to protect yourself. You don't want to end up in Yuma. Right?"

Rawlins thought it over.

"But even a woman?"

"*Especially* a woman."

Rawlins looked up questioningly.

Brady smiled.

"Women make the best witnesses."

There was a sudden shuffling sound from above, up on the cabin's roof. Both men froze, and Brady lifted his shotgun off the table. Then he listened carefully, as a very uneasy Rawlins rose from his chair and pulled a .38 from his belt. They waited motionless in the ensuing silence.

Even Brady seemed spooked.

But he was ready, at any minute, to fire his shotgun through the cabin roof.

Suddenly, there was a loud scraping sound within the large stone fireplace, as the limp and bound body of McCoy crashed feet-first to the bottom of the stone fireplace. Both men were naturally astonished, and Rawlins instinctively moved toward his seemingly-dead friend.

Which was my cue.

I smashed the barrel of my Winchester through the window and stuck the end of the barrel right into the back of Rawlins's neck.

He froze.

At the same time, Jack stepped into the room from the front door-way and stared at Brady, who immediately swung around his shotgun to fire.

It was a bad move.

Jack drew his Colt and shot Brady in the left thigh.

Where else?

Brady immediately dropped his double-barrel and slumped down to the floor holding his bleeding leg as Coyote and Red Star, now off the roof, entered the room behind Jack.

It was over.

I withdrew my rifle from the window, walked around the front of the cabin, and entered the room.

Rawlins, terrified, had now backed into the far wall of the cabin.

"Hands up," Jack said.

The miner did as he was told.

Then Jack lifted his Colt and fired five instantaneous shots into the cabin wall around Rawlins's head.

It was quite a warning.

"You sure you want to rob banks?" he asked.

When the terrified Rawlins didn't respond, Jack continued.

"I understand you're a miner."

Rawlins nodded.

"It's honest work."

He nodded again.

At the same time, Red Star walked over to the fireplace and pulled out McCoy who was starting to revive a bit. Then John took a basin of water from the table and dumped it over McCoy's face. Then he cut his bonds and helped him up.

McCoy was now standing next to Rawlins, and the two wary young miners looked at Jack.

"You going to cause any more trouble?" he asked.

They both shook their heads "no."

"Driscoll says he'll take you back."

They both nodded again.

"You can go," Jack said. "But watch the newspapers. Your friend Brady will hang in Prescott in a few weeks."

The two grateful miners left immediately.

Now Jack turned his attention back to Brady.

The murderer was still sitting on the bloody floor in a lot of pain. He seemed disinterested in everything else that had happened since the shooting.

Jack looked down at the man and spoke coldly.

"Look up at me."

Brady looked up.

Jack warned him.

"If I hear a word from you before we get to Prescott, I'll kill you on the spot."

Which I knew wasn't true, but Brady didn't know it.

"Do you understand me?" Jack said.

Brady nodded weakly, but Jack still wasn't satisfied. He immediately kicked the man sharply in his wounded thigh, and Brady cried out, whimpered, and cringed.

"I certainly hope so," Jack said.

[Jim Ellis]

Chapter 27

Jackson Ranch

Saturday, July 4th

It was a nice spread in a quiet valley east of Prescott.

Mr. Jackson must have seen us coming since he was waiting outside the main house.

I was trailing behind Jack and John, leading Brady's horse since he was helplessly bound to his saddle.

Dan Jackson looked to be in his late sixties, a rugged rancher who'd ridden with Matthias Shannon and Grey Wolf back in the day.

He was clearly happy to see the two sons of his old compadres.

"Welcome, boys!"

We pulled up in front of him.

Amused, he looked over at Brady, who hadn't said a word since Jack had punctured his thigh in the mountain cabin.

"Another one?" Jackson kidded.

Jack smiled as well.

"They all seem to be shot in the same leg," the old rancher pointed out.

"Well, we do our best," Jack kidded back. "We try to deter the criminal mind from speculating about future transgressions."

Jackson nodded.

He looked up at me.

"His friends," he explained, "are waiting back at the stables."

Meaning Stark and Rodriquez.

Then he turned back to Jack and John.

"Come on in boys! Judith's cooking up a feast!"

Which it certainly was!

Later that evening, after the roast and the potatoes and the greens and the gravy and all the rest of it, Mrs. Jackson brought out the birthday cake. It was a yummy-looking sourdough with red, white, and blue icing, with a little American flag stuck in the middle.

With thirty-eight stars.

It was July 4th.

It was Jack's birthday.

It was also Independence Day from the bloody British.

Normally, back at Rising Sun, there'd be a big celebration with music and dancing and fireworks, but this year things would have to be delayed until we returned.

Old Man Jackson rose at the head of the table and made a toast.

He was definitely feeling his whiskey.

"Happy Birthday to Matthias's second son, of whom he'd be very proud."

We drank to the toast.

Mrs. J., Red Star, Dark Sky, and me.

Coyote was out in the stalls minding our other "guests."

Mr. J. continued.

"As well as an anticipatory toast to the upcoming birthday of Grey Wolf's boy, of whom he'd also be very proud."

We drank again.

Then the old man looked over at Jack.

"Say something, son."

Jack stood up at his place at the table, looking first at Mrs. Jackson."

"Thank you, ma'am, for the perfect birthday meal and the perfect birthday dessert."

But he wasn't finished.

"And happy birthday to the independent union of states, and the hope that the nation's flag will soon have another star."

We toasted again, and me and the old man even cheered a bit.

I guess I was getting a bit loopy myself.

Then Dark Sky handed Jack a small blue envelope.

"It's a birthday present," he clarified.

Jack was surprised, even confused, so Dark Sky explained.

"It's from Moonlight, Jack. She asked me to give it to you on your birthday."

Jack took the envelope and tucked it inside his vest.

"Open it!" Jackson blustered, and since everyone agreed, Jack took it out again and opened it up.

Inside was a small photograph.

"She had it taken in Tucson," Dark Sky further explained.

"Well, let's have a look, Jack," Jackson insisted.

So Jack passed it around the table until it finally made its way to me. I must say, I was taken back a bit. I knew Moonlight pretty well from the corral, but I still considered her a young girl, but the photograph revealed a remarkably beautiful young woman, wearing traditional Papago clothes, with a beaded headband around her long black hair. She was so beautiful that I'm surprised she didn't crack the camera in Tucson, and I nearly said so, but I caught myself.

I turned it over. Maybe I shouldn't have, but I did. It said, "Happy Birthday, Jack!" in neat black letters, signed, "Your Moonlight."

I didn't know what to make of the "your," so I decided to think about it tomorrow when I was completely sober, then I handed the photograph back to Jack.

It was hard to read him, of course.

It usually is.

It was hard to fathom the *meaning* of all of it.

Jack looked over at Dark Sky.

"I'm very grateful," he said simply, then he tucked the picture back inside his vest.

Later that night, after too much drink, Old Man Jackson was telling fantastical stories about the old days.

"Then we could see," he remembered dramatically, "as that long-haired bastard came up behind her, knocked her to the ground, and put a knife to her throat. Grey Wolf and I were too far away to do anything, so I stopped where I was, expecting the worst."

"Then," he continued with a flourish, "your old man, who was even farther away than me and Grey Wolf, shot him right through the forehead at eight hundred yards!"

Which sounded impossible to me.

Which sounded like the whiskey had added several hundred yards to his memory, but I didn't have to say a word. Jackson had already read my mind. He knew what I was thinking.

Dark Sky too.

"Dammit!" he affirmed. "It wasn't a single foot less than eight hundred yards! And I don't care if it's believed or not. I was there!"

John, who seldom spoke, decided to reassure the old man.

"If it was Jack's father, it could have been nine hundred yards."

Which seemed even more preposterous, but Jackson clearly liked it, and he leaned over the table and struck it with his fist.

"Well said, young man!"

Then he sat back into his chair and grew even more nostalgic.

"I sure miss those days when I rode out with your fathers."

There was silence in the room.

But not for long.

"And now *you* boys," he continued, "are riding out together, doing the same things, cleaning scum from the territory."

We all appreciated it.

Then Mrs. J. appeared in the doorway and gave her husband a look. It was a loving look, but it was also one of those "that's enough of that for one night, my dear" looks.

He didn't resist.

"Yes, my love."

He stood up and looked down at us all.

"I'll see you boys in the morning."

After he left the room, Red Star and Dark Sky also left, as Mrs. Jackson stepped over to me and Jack.

She looked down at Jack.

"This was forwarded from Rising Sun."

She handed Jack a much-traveled letter, then she left the room.

Now it was just me and Jack.

He looked at the letter, and he looked at me.

"Maybe you should marry White Dove, Jim," he said.

Which I certainly wasn't expecting.

Then he stood up and left the room.

The letter, of course, had come from back east. From his girl back east. From Miss Jennifer Cameron of New Brunswick, New Jersey, who'd sent him a photo in her previous letter.

Who was also very beautiful.

In a different kind of way.

In an eastern kind of way.

It made me grateful that my own life was so simple. Driving herd and loving pretty White Dove.

I felt sorry for Jack, but I never said a word about it.

Never.

[Jim Ellis]

Chapter 28

The Stalls

Saturday, July 4th

I was on watch that night.

In the horse barn.

At the stalls.

Nothing much was happening, and nothing much would.

It was quiet and dark, except for my single kerosene lamp.

I sat on a bale of hay with my Winchester ready nearby.

I was tired, but I was alert.

When I heard the footsteps, I lifted my Winchester.

Jack emerged from the outer darkness into the old barn.

He nodded at me, and I lowered my rifle and nodded back. To let him know that everything was fine. Naturally, I was wondering what he was still doing up in the middle of the night.

I wondered if Moonlight's photograph had set him to thinking about her. And about that girl back east. Jim and I wondered about it from time to time, but we never said a word to either Jack or Red Star.

"All quiet," I said.

"Good. Let's take a look."

I stood up, picked up my lantern, and we walked over to the first stall together.

When I held the lantern high above the wooden gate, we looked down at Rodriquez who was sleeping soundly despite being manacled to the floor.

Then we did the same thing at the next stall, where Brady, also chained, also slept in silence.

Then we went to the third stall.

As soon as I lifted the light, we could see the glaring eyes of Damien Stark staring back at us, as if waiting for us. He sat in the far corner of the stall with his back against the wall. Like the others, he was chained and bandaged, but he was also defiant.

Malevolent.

He smiled at Jack.

His voice was cold and harsh and vicious.

"I don't know who you are, kid, or what's going on, so I'm not saying a word. But I can tell you one thing. Nothing will ever happen to me."

I wondered if Jack would respond.

He did, dismissively.

"Tell it in court."

"I'll never go to court, kid. *Never.*"

He let it sink in, then he continued.

"Do you know why I'm sitting up in the darkness? What I'm thinking about?"

Jack gave no response.

"I'm thinking about the ways to watch you die. How I'll mutilate your face and the rest of you when you're cold and dead."

Jack walked away.

Unperturbed.

I lowered my lamp, casting Stark into the darkness once again.

Jack gave me another nod, as he walked out of the barn into his own darkness.

Until his footsteps faded away.

It gave me a lot to think about.

[Dark Sky]

Chapter 29

Prescott

Tuesday, July 7th

I knew something was wrong.

Right away.

As soon as we entered the town.

I'm not really sure *how* I knew, but I did.

Twilight was falling, the business day in the capital was over, and there were only a few people on the main street. The capital looked like it always did, except for all the signs about the upcoming election.

"LAW, ORDER, & SHANNON!"
"VOTE SHANNON: SHANNON MEANS STATEHOOD!"

Etc.

All blue and white.

As well as:

"VOTE MITCHELL: EXPERIENCE & LEADERSHIP."
"MITCHELL'S YOUR MAN!"

Etc.

All red.

There was more red than blue.

Jim and I came down the street leading our three prisoners who were bound on horseback.

Coyote trailed.

Jack and Dark Sky had come into town earlier in the afternoon.

Jack took a room with a view of the street at the Sheridan Hotel, across from the Sheriff's office, and Dark Sky hung around on the street nearby, inconspicuous but alert.

Some of the locals stopped to take a quick look at us leading the prisoners along, but, in general, it was nothing more than a casual attention. There was little recognition. No fuss.

As we approached the sheriff's office, I could see Jack in the window of his hotel room. The barrel of his Winchester was also visible. Dark Sky was sitting over near a hitching post.

Everything went smoothly, but I was still uneasy.

When we pulled up, Jim and I dismounted and went inside.

A deputy, maybe thirty years old, was sitting at the desk. When we entered, he looked out the window and saw the prisoners waiting on horseback guarded by Coyote's shotgun.

He was surprised.

So was I.

I was expecting that Lewis Brackden, the Prescott sheriff, would be waiting for us, ready to take custody of the prisoners. From all reports, Brackden was a tough reliable man, around forty, who was good with a gun. Which is why he was brought in from Abilene to enforce the law in the capital city.

"Who's that?" the deputy asked.

"Who are you?" I asked.

"Evan Conrad."

"Where's Brackden?"

"He's out of town on business."

Something was wrong.

I put the posters down on the desk in front of the deputy. I wanted him to realize that this was serious. Not just some Indian and a cowboy bringing in a few rustlers.

The posters definitely got his attention.

He stood up, walked to the window, and stared out at the three exhausted murderers.

"Weren't you warned?" I asked.

It was clear that he hadn't been. He had no idea what was going on.

"Is that *really* the three of them?"

He seemed incredulous.

"Yes."

"Is that *really* Damien Stark?"

"Yes, and I'd like to get them off the street as fast as possible."

He understood, and he snapped out of it.

He seemed excited.

"Of course! Of course! Bring them in! Bring them in!"

Which we did without incident.

The Prescott Jail consisted of two small cells in the back of the sheriff's office. We put Stark in one, and the other two in the other cell.

I looked at Conrad.

I was concerned.

"It looks like you're all alone here."

It was a question.

"Yes. But I'll be fine."

I wasn't so sure.

"When does Brackden get back?"

"I'm not sure, maybe in a couple of days."

I certainly didn't like the sound of that.

[John Red Star]

Chapter 30

Chapel

Tuesday, July 7th

Late that night, in the middle of the night, Jack went to the little chapel at the edge of town.

He told John Red Star, who told me.

I know that chapel.

It's a little white adobe dedicated to the Sacred Heart. Inside, it's very simple. Spanish, Mexican, with white walls, a small fresco of the Madonna, a tiny stone altar, a wooden carved statue of the Sacred Heart, etc. It was erected back in the early days of Prescott for riders coming in and out of town. In time, it was superseded by other larger churches, but the town never tore it down.

It remained a comfort station for the weary.

That night it was empty, lit with white votive lights.

Jack sat on the second bench of three in front of the statue. In front of the Sacred Heart.

I suppose he might have been emotionally exhausted.

Jack Shannon, except for his smile, had a habit of never really revealing very much about himself, except to Red Star, except maybe in prayer.

I'm told that he sat there for several hours, mostly in silence.

"Did he say anything?" I asked Red Star.

"Yes, not much."

"What?"

"Four words."

"What?"

"It's done."

Which was two words, which I did my best to understand.

I suppose that Jack was hoping that what he'd done had been done in the right way and that his actions would be justified in the eyes of the Lord. Maybe he was also saying that he was done with gunplay, that all he really wanted to do was ride back to Rising Sun and be a rancher like his father. Maybe he was saying, it's done, and now I'm ready to put it all behind me.

All of it.

Maybe he was also saying, it's done, and now I need some guidance about some other things, some important things, about the girl back east and the girl back here in Rising Sun. Maybe he was saying, it's done, meaning all the law-and-order stuff, and now it was time to put the rest of his life in order. It was time to face what he'd been avoiding.

Maybe he was saying that now that *that's* done, I need some help deciding what to do next, which won't be easy.

Maybe I'm wrong.

All wrong.

Maybe I'm reading too much into two simple words.

Red Star was no help at all.

"What else?" I asked.

He told me the other two words.

"I'm trying."

Which I believe needs no explication.

[Padre Luis Delgado]

Chapter 31

Assembly Hall

Wednesday, July 8th

I was stunned!

Of course, I was!

Stunned!

"All of them?" I asked in disbelief.

"Yes."

The kid had done exactly what he'd said he would do.

I was standing alone in the Assembly Hall of the territorial congress. A session had ended about an hour ago, and I was finishing up some paperwork at Edward's desk. They came in behind me.

The kid in his rancher blacks and an impressive-looking Indian in buckskin.

I knew, of course, that the Shannons had a long and comfortable history with the Papagos down near the border, but I'd never seen one in the Assembly Hall before.

I suppose I take the building for granted, but the Prescott Assembly Hall is very impressive. Like the Courthouse, it's a showcase for a territory that's striving to become a state. It's our symbol of democracy and civilization out here on the western frontier. It's much larger than one might expect, with white desks, dark woods, and tastefully gilt decor. Above the speaker's podium, there's a large striking portrait of Washington dressed in his military regalia, based on the famous Peale portrait. Off to one side of the portrait is an American Flag. Off to the other side is our Territorial Flag.

Neither Jack nor the Indian showed any response to their present surroundings. They were all business. But I did catch Jack taking a long look up at Washington, whom I later learned was his personal hero. Apparently, when he was at school back east, he went to the Morristown encampment and the Monmouth Battlefield.

"Yes," Jack said, "they're locked in the city jail, awaiting trial."

I didn't know what to say, so I said what I felt.

"You're a remarkable young man, Jack."

"I had help."

He introduced me to his companion, and we shook hands.

His name was John Red Star.

"How much do you think it will help?" Jack asked.

He was referring to the election.

"I think it'll make the difference."

"Do you think Edward will be able to get things done in Washington?"

"I do, Jack, I really do."

I meant it.

Then Edward returned to the chamber. He'd obviously heard what had happened and that Jack was looking for him.

He was a combination of amazement and relief.

"Thank goodness you're all right!" he said.

Then he shook hands warmly with both his brother and Red Star.

"Was anyone hurt?" he asked with concern."

"Dark Sky was hit in the arm, but he's doing fine."

"It's a miracle, Jack!"

I felt the same way.

"Whitson believes you can win the election," Jack said to his older brother.

"I have no doubt! Thanks to the two of you."

The kid just nodded, then he spoke again.

"You know what needs to be done, Edward."

"Of course, Jack! Law, order, and statehood. We'll get all three. I guarantee it!"

But Jack still had another concern that he needed to address.

"Why wasn't the jail ready last night?"

Edward was shocked.

He looked over at me.

I was equally confused.

I didn't understand.

"Wasn't the sheriff there?" I asked.

"No."

Edward was furious.

"That damned Brackden! Where the hell was he?"

I didn't know, so Jack explained.

"We were told that he's out of town on business."

Edward was angry and frustrated, and so was I.

"We'll look into it, Jack," he promised, "and I'll send another man to help out Conrad until Brackden gets back."

Jack seemed satisfied.

Somewhat satisfied.

"Are the courts ready?" he asked.

"Absolutely," I assured him.

"We have depositions," Jack explained, "signed confessions, and a witness list,"

Red Star handed me the documents.

"Perfect, they'll be *no* problems, Jack. I'll make sure of it," I assured him.

"Good."

Edward looked at his brother again.

"You've done something quite remarkable, Jack. The both of you."

Jack said nothing, neither did Red Star.

"Will you be sticking around?" Edward asked.

"Yes, until they hang."

"Good."

But Edward couldn't resist asking another question.

"Did you really beat Stark up and up?"

"Yes."

I was amazed all over again.

"Was it close?" Edward asked.

"No."

ARIZONA SUNDOWN

[Philip Whitson]

197

Chapter 32

Courthouse

Wednesday, July 15th

The capital courthouse was packed.

The gavel came down, and everyone went silent. Judge Bentham looked down at the already convicted prisoner, Luis Rodriquez.

A court official rose.

"The prisoner will rise."

Rodriquez stood up. All his bravado was gone. He was a silent broken man fully aware of his destiny, maybe silently trying to make his peace with God.

Maybe not.

The judge was direct and stern.

"It is the judgment and sentence of this court that in retribution for the heinous and cold-blooded crimes already confessed to, that you be taken hence in secure confinement until Saturday, the twenty-fifth day of July, 1885, and that upon that day, just before sundown, you be taken into the open courtyard adjacent to the Prescott City Jail and there be hung by the neck until you are dead."

The crowd was spellbound.

So was I.

The judge paused, then finished.

"And may God have mercy on your venomous soul."

There was nothing but silence in the room.

The gavel struck once more.

[Philip Whitson]

Chapter 33

New York Sun

Thursday, July 16th

It seemed quite useless to me, but I did it anyway.

My father set it up.

At the time, my father was city editor at the *Sun*, and he was good friends with William "Bill" Stockton, who was one of the paper's two national editors. Specifically the one who oversaw WOTM news. Meaning "West of the Mississippi." Stockton had lived out west for twenty years, first covering the California Gold Rush for the *Sun*, then, years later, covering the Lincoln County War in New Mexico, until he was run out of the territory by the Santa Fe Ring. He'd known John Chisum, and Billy Bonney, and John C. Fremont, and Leland Stanford, and many other notable figures on the western frontier.

He was also a great storyteller. Maybe a bit of a blowhard, but certainly a likeable one. When I was a kid, he'd regularly mesmerize me with his tales of the old West, but I wasn't so sure about our meeting today.

About a month ago, I went to my old man.

"Jennifer wants to talk to Mr. Stockton."

He was surprised, so I clarified.

"She wants to see what he knows about the Shannons and about Rising Sun."

He understood.

He'd met my Rutgers roommate Jack Shannon, and he was aware that Jennifer hadn't heard from him since he'd left New Brunswick over a month earlier.

He was also my cousin Jennifer's godfather as well as her favorite uncle, and he was willing to do anything she wanted.

"Fine, let me talk to Bill."

Which he did, and Stockton, who was willing to talk to anyone about anything, said "Sure, I know a bit about the Shannons, but give me a month or so to check out a few things."

Now it was a month later.

Jennifer and I sat silently in the comfortable taxi-hansom as it made its way through the busy Manhattan streets towards the city's publishing district. It was a pleasant summer day, and the streets were full of busy businessmen, clerks, secretaries, and occasional fashionable women, all bustling about the great metropolis. Jennifer, in one of her lovely white dresses, looked out the window as we arrived at the entrance of the *Sun*'s editorial offices.

Soon we were entering the cluttered office of William Stockton, who was expecting us.

Stockton was probably sixty or so. A big man, somewhat worn, with too much girth, with a neatly-trimmed beard.

He rose immediately as I introduced Jennifer.

"This is my cousin, Miss Jennifer Cameron, Mr. Stockton."

He greeted her formally and, with a flourish, offered her a chair.

Then he shook my hand.

"Good to see you, kid."

Then he sat back down behind his desk.

"Jennifer," I reminded him, "has a few questions."

"Of course, she does. My pleasure."

He looked directly at Jennifer and gave her his full attention.

"I greatly appreciate your time, Mr. Stockton."

"Anytime, young lady."

She got right to it.

"I'm wondering what you might know about John Shannon of Rising Sun Ranch in Arizona Territory."

"To be honest, I know very little about the young man himself, but I know a fair amount about his father. Matthias Shannon was one of those distinguished pioneers, like Hooker and Vail, who brought a determination for honesty and decency into the young territory."

"Tell me about it."

Which he did.

"Matthias Shannon came out of Missouri somewhere, served in the US calvary, and was down there with Jackson at New Orleans. Later, he went west to find his fortune as a horse breeder and trader. Then, and I'm not exactly sure how it happened, he became good friends with an Indian warrior chief named Grey Wolf. A Papago. With whom he became, according to what I've heard, a blood-brother."

"What's that?"

He smiled.

"I have no idea, Jennifer, but I like the sound of it."

Stockton reached over and lifted up a small tumbler from his crowded desktop and sipped at the purple. My father told me that he sipped blackberry brandy throughout the afternoons, then he switched to scotch in the evenings.

Which sounded pretty disgusting to me.

"They somehow got the Mexican land rights to a small valley in southern Arizona near the Sauceda Mountains, where they built a Ranch together. The Indian, as it turned out, was much more than just a warrior. He'd been educated by the Franciscans, and he was apparently highly adept at engineering, and he immediately built a remarkable reservoir and irrigation system to water the valley. Which prospered."

"Who was there?"

"Mostly Papagos, reputedly a peaceful border tribe, who were mostly farmers, along with a bunch of Mexican ranch hands. All of whom were Catholic, by the way. Irish Matthias Shannon, the vaqueros, and the Indians."

He looked at Jennifer.

"What are you, my dear?"

It seemed remarkably rude, especially since he knew about Jennifer's uncertain relationship with Jack, but she didn't seem to mind. I suppose it seemed like the least of her problems.

"The same. Catholic."

"Good," he said, as if that solved her problems.

As for Stockton himself, my old man once told me that "Bill believes in nothing but the American flag."

"So they raised quality horses," he continued, "along with a sizable herd, maybe a thousand or so at the upper end, and they mostly kept to themselves. Mostly."

"Were they violent men?"

"Of course. Whenever they had to be. I heard they rode out many times against rustlers, robbers, raiding Navahos, and renegade Apaches. I've even heard that Grey Wolf and Matthias once had a run-in with Cochise himself. It was in a ravine somewhere, completely by chance, when they came upon Cochise and five other Apache braves, and it certainly looked bad for Shannon and his Indian friend. Did I mention that the Apache and the Papago are traditional enemies?"

Neither Jennifer nor I responded, so Stockton proceeded.

"So Matthias figured that he should try something, anything, so he said, I suppose in English, 'You go your way, and we'll go ours,' and that's exactly what happened. They passed each other without another word."

[There is, as far as I know, no collaborative evidence to support this story. – E.R.]

"Were they killers?" Jennifer asked.

I remember thinking to myself at the time that maybe *this* is why she'd come here today. After all, Jennifer and I had both seen what Jack could do with a gun.

Stockton shrugged.

"I suppose whenever it was necessary, young lady. It's how the frontiers are civilized. I feel confident in saying that there's not a single spot of God's great earth that doesn't have its own bloody history. Ever since Cain bludgeoned his brother. Ever since Cain said to the Lord, 'I know not; am I my brother's keeper.' Ever since the Lord sayeth, 'What hast thou done? The voice of thy brother's blood crieth to me from the earth.'"

Which wasn't very helpful at all.

Stockton took another sip, actually a rather healthy gulp.

I remembered my father once saying, "Did you ever notice that non-believers like to cite the scriptures with both remarkable recollection and fluidity?"

Stockton wasn't finished.

"Think of your own state, my dear, and all the blood that was shed in the founding of colonial New Jersey by the Dutch, the Swedes, the English, the Scots, the Quakers, and the Lenape Indians. And all the rest of them. Similarly, were not many of the most important battles of our war for independence fought on New Jersey soil?"

Stockton stopped, as if admiring his own elegant soliloquy. Then he tried to tie it all together.

"From what I know, the Shannons only used their weapons in the cause of righteousness. I assume that that's the same for the young man you love."

I was shocked by the old idiot's presumption and his indiscrete usage of the word "love," but Jennifer seemed to appreciate his honesty.

She nodded thoughtfully.

"Have I gone too far?" he asked.

"Not at all."

"Then let me put it this way, it seems to me that Matthias Shannon and Grey Wolf lived as Christians in a violent land and often felt it necessary to assert their foundational beliefs regarding justice."

He took another sip.

"What about politics?" Jennifer asked, which surprised me.

Did she and Jack talk about such things?

"They avoided it," Stockton explained, "doing their best to keep their valley neutral, but Matthias did make at least one trip east to use his considerable influence with President Grant on behalf of the Indian situation in southern Arizona and elsewhere."

Then Stockton remembered something else.

"I'm sure you already know that Matthias's older son is currently the territory's Attorney General and that he's running to come to Washington as Arizona's only delegate. I met him once in Albuquerque. A very friendly type."

"And Jack?"

"Nope, never met him. Supposedly, he's a lot more like his father. He's the son of Matthias's second wife, a Brazilian lady who died when Jack was a young boy."

In case Jennifer didn't know, I felt I should clarify.

"His mother was half Portuguese and half Irish, living in Rio de Janeiro when she first met Matthias."

"Yes," Stockton agreed, "and killed by a rattler."

Which Jennifer didn't know.

"Killed by a snake?" she asked uneasily.

"Yes, ma'am."

Our little conference seemed to be getting more and more unproductive, and I wondered if I should get Jennifer out of there as fast as I could.

"Do you love him that much?" Stockton asked, with an obvious paucity of tact, but with discernable concern.

"He hasn't written. He hasn't answered any of my letters."

"It's possible that he might not have received those letters, Jennifer. The mails out west can be highly sporadic."

He was trying to help.

"It's been over two months."

Stockton thought it over.

"Can I be honest, Jennifer?"

Which made me nervous.

"Of course. Please do, no one else will."

Which I suppose was directed at both me and her parents.

Stockton tried to be gentle about it.

I'll give him credit for that at least.

"I don't know the young boy, Jennifer, and I have no idea what will happen, but you need to prepare yourself for the worst. He's a different kind of boy than Erick here. He's a western boy who's been raised in the spirit of his father. Men like that *do*, they don't procrastinate, and I'm fearful that your relationship might be over."

It was deadly, and I was furious with the old fool, but Jennifer seemed to appreciate his candor.

She stood up and extended her hand.

"Thank you for your kindness, Mr. Stockton."

He took her hand and nodded like she was the Countess of Buchan.

"I hope that I'm wrong," he said. "It wouldn't be the first time, my dear."

No argument there.

I immediately escorted Jennifer out of his office.

I said nothing to Stockton because I was afraid that I might say something I'd regret.

Outside in the hallway, I looked at Jennifer, who was trying to be brave.

"Are you all right?" I asked foolishly.

She looked at me and answered honestly.

"I'm very unhappy, Erick."

Which, of course, made me unhappy as well, as I held her and comforted her within my arms.

[Erick Ramsey]

Chapter 34

Courthouse

Friday, July 17th

Again.

"The prisoner will rise."

Brady stood up before the packed courthouse. Despite his lingering wound and his current situation, he'd regained his defiant demeanor.

He looked around at the crowd.

Coldly.

Judge Bentham ignored him.

"It's the considered judgment and sentence of this court that in recompense for the unspeakable crimes committed and admitted, you be held in secure confinement until the twenty-fifth day of July, 1885, and that upon that day, just before sundown, you'll be taken into the open courtyard adjacent to the Prescott City Jail, there to be hung by the neck until you are dead."

All the while Brady glared at a man seated across the courthouse. It was Elisha Holt, the bank officer at the Globe branch of Central Arizona Bank who'd survived Brady's assaults last year, and who'd given withering witness in court earlier in the afternoon. Despite Brady's hateful looks, the man was entirely unfazed and unintimidated.

Realizing that he was having no effect, Brady feigned disinterest.

"And may God have mercy on your blackened soul."

The gavel came down.

[Philip Whitson]

Chapter 35

Jennifer's Third Letter

Friday, July 17th

Dear Jack,

Please write.

I've been told about your family, and more about Rising Sun, and a bit about you.

In truth, I don't care about anything except loving you. I often find myself weak with fears and loneliness, and I believe that my family questions my sanity.

Why is the world so dark?

What's wrong, my Jack?

Where is my darling?

Your love forever, Jennifer

Editor's Summary

Friday, July 17th

According to various newspaper accounts, late on July 17th, the notorious gunman Damien Stark escaped from the Prescott City Jail, where he was awaiting his upcoming trial for several murders perpetrated in Arizona Territory, most specifically the cold-blooded murders of Judge Jonathan Dolan and US Marshal Charles Caldwell in the small town of Benson, Arizona, three months ago.

An unknown associate of Stark's apparently entered the jailhouse late that night and immediately incapacitated the guard on duty, Deputy Evan Conrad, who was knocked unconscious. Then the intruder quickly released Stark from his cell, gave him his holster and .45, and both men exited the building together into a northside alleyway where two saddled horses were waiting.

But the men were surprised by Edward Shannon, territorial District Attorney, currently running for Arizona congressional delegate in the upcoming election. Mr. Shannon, a distinguished lawyer and jurist, seems to have been notified about a possible jailbreak, and he took it upon himself to stand guard outside the jailhouse that night, armed with a Smith & Wesson Model 3.

When Shannon confronted the two men, gunfire exchanged. Shannon struck and killed Stark's accomplice, a man now identified as Hank Yolt, but the District Attorney was similarly killed by Damien Stark who, uncharacteristically, shot him with his left hand since his right hand had been severely injured during his arrest in Elfrida last May.

Fortunately, in the meantime, Deputy Conrad had roused himself from his blow to the head, and when he heard the shots discharged, he rushed out to the alleyway with his shotgun and got the drop on Damien Stark. Then he led the murderer back into the city jailhouse and incarcerated him once again into his cell.

In order to prevent any delay regarding the upcoming murder trial of Damien Stark, the Territorial Governor, Frederick Tritle, has decided not to additionally indict Stark for the murder of Edward Shannon. The governor has, however, reserved the right to make such an indictment in the future if necessary.

At present, the entire territory mourns the tragic death of heroic Edward Shannon and looks forward to the conviction and eventual hanging of Damien Stark.

Chapter 36

Courthouse

Thursday, July 23rd

Once again.

"The prisoner will rise."

He did.

Damien Stark, the most hated man in Arizona Territory, stood before the packed courthouse. He looked directly forward, seemingly staring at nothing. Immobile. As if unable to comprehend how he'd ended up where he'd ended up.

The judge spoke loudly and firm.

"It is the judgment and sentence of this court . . ."

As his sentence was pronounced, Stark turned and looked over into the side gallery. So did I. Jack Shannon was standing there holding a Winchester.

In silence.

Impassive.

Then Stark looked away, forward again.

Defeated.

I'd like to believe that I'm neither a hateful man nor a vindictive man, but I was on that day, and I thanked the Lord in the recesses of my heart for the justice that would soon be coming at the end of the rope.

"May God, if he's able, have mercy on your feculent soul."

Gavel.

Cheers.

[Philip Whitson]

Chapter 37

Jack's Letter

Friday, July 24th

[Written on Sheridan Hotel stationary, Prescott, Arizona]

Dear Jennifer,

I've decided not to return east in the fall, and I feel certain that you shouldn't wait for my return beyond that time.

Please try to forgive me.

I've never lied to you about my feelings, or about anything else, but certain complications in Arizona have left me confused and uncertain.

I'm aware that this letter is entirely unsatisfactory, but it accurately reflects my present state of mind.

I think of you, Jennifer, as a most marvelous young woman, one to be upheld, admired, and loved. It's now best that you forget me, and hopefully forgive me as well.

Jack

Chapter 38

Murray's Saloon

Saturday, July 25th

The place was empty.

Murray's was pretty much like every other saloon in the territory, with mirrors, an oak backbar, and a large painting of a barely dressed woman of dubious character, although, I must admit, far less lascivious than most. What was different about Murray's today was that it was empty on an early evening on a pleasant Saturday in the month of July.

It was just me, Jack, and Red Star.

As well as an old bearded barkeep who kept himself busy at the far end of the counter, respecting our silence.

We'd buried Edward five days ago. Ashes to Ashes. Rest in peace. Within the Catholic cemetery at the edge of town. Jack had done his best to keep it quiet since he knew that the whole town would have shown up to pay their respects. But Jack wanted to keep it simple, and the priest agreed, so it was just the three of us.

In silence.

As we'd been for most of the past five days.

As we were now.

Standing at the cherry-wood bar.

Jack and me with whiskey shots waiting in front of us on the counter. John with an untouched seltzer.

What was there to say anyway?

What was there to do except stare at the clock?

7:18.

7:19.

I do remember trying to fathom what Jack might be thinking.

Which was pointless.

I remember staring rather mindlessly at the lightly floating dead motes as they swirled within a shaft of the twilight from one of the side windows.

As for Edward's death, the newspapers didn't get it exactly right because John had also been there that night, and he'd taken a bullet through his left shoulder in the effort to get Stark back into his jail cell. I wasn't there, but I saw his wound later that night when the local doc patched him up. It was a mess, and I'm sure painful as hell.

"Will he be all right?" Jack asked the doc.

"Maybe. But he'll need some time to heal, and it'll hurt a lot. Like hell."

As for Red Star, he never mentioned it.

He also never mentioned whatever happened that night.

Neither did Jack.

Edward was dead, Stark was back in jail, and there was nothing more to say about it.

Just sadness.

Just loss.

To make things worse, General Grant had died two days previous at his Mount McGregor cottage in upstate New York. President Cleveland had ordered a thirty-day national period of mourning and plans were being made for the funeral and an appropriate monument. I was fully aware that Jack's father had once met with President Grant, and that the Rising Sun Papagos revered the man for his efforts to delegate and negotiate a fair-minded future for the nation's Indian tribes.

Thus death was very much in the air.

With more to come.

Then a man wearing his best Sunday suit hurried down the interior stairway. He was surprised to see customers, and equally surprised to see his bartender.

"Howard! It's almost sundown. Shut the place down!"

The old man wasn't interested.

"I don't care much to go, Mr. Sheridan."

"Well, do whatever you like. I'll be back later."

Then he rushed out the front doors of his saloon, rushing up the street.

It was quiet again.

The bartender came over to explain himself.

"It's a necessary thing, of course," he said, "but like you fellas, I don't really care to see it."

He noticed that John's glass was untouched.

"Something else?" he checked.

"I'm fine," John said, so the old man nodded and went back to his business at the end of the bar.

Then John spoke again.

To me and Jack.

"It'll be good to get back home."

Jack agreed.

"Yeah, I'll be glad to forget about Prescott."

Who could blame him?

Then we heard some noise from up the street, like a crowd milling around, or maybe starting to disperse.

7:26.

"Well, that'll be it," the old man said.

Jack looked down at his unfinished drink and decided to leave it. He dropped a few coins on the counter, nodded at the barkeep, and the three of us left through the front door.

We mounted right outside.

It must have hurt Red Star quite a bit to get up in his saddle, but he didn't show it. Then Jack directed Night south, out of town, and we followed.

John looked back once.

Jack never did.

Well, you can bet that I did!

The three of them were dangling there in the twilight, high on their scaffolds above the large milling crowd.

Stark, Brady, and Rodriquez.

All dead.

Three murderers.

It felt good.

Maybe it shouldn't have, but it did.

Then we headed home.

Into a wide and reddish-purple Arizona sundown.

[Jim Ellis]

Chapter 39

Rising Sun

Sunday, July 26th

Yeah, it was good to be back home.

John's wound had been festering a bit with infectus, and his shirt was soaked through at the left shoulder and red with blood.

Now he could rest.

Now Running Brook could tend to his wound.

Coyote and Dark Sky were waiting on the front porch.

Eliza, the young Mormon girl, was there as well.

Everyone at Rising Sun already knew about Edward's death, and there was sadness in the air.

A sense of mourning, which overwhelmed the homecoming.

When we got closer, Dark Sky spotted the blood.

"He's been hit!"

I looked over at Red Star who definitely looked a bit woozy, which I hadn't noticed before. I guess the hot sun and the long ride hadn't done him much good.

As we pulled up, John slipped slowly from his saddle into Coyote's arms. Then Coyote and Dark Sky helped him inside the house.

Eliza just sat there terrified.

She looked up at Jack.

"Can I help?"

"I'm sure he'd like that."

She stood up immediately, ready to follow the others into the house.

She looked lovely in her pretty yellow dress.

Then she looked back at Jack.

"Will he be all right?"

"Yes, he'll be all right."

She hesitated, then she asked what she'd been wanting to ask.

"I'd like to stay here at Rising Sun."

He understood.

"That won't be a problem."

She smiled and quickly went into the house.

[Jim Ellis]

Corral

Sunday, July 26th

I knew they were back, but I decided to wait at the stables rather than the big house.

After all, the corral was *our* place.

With the horses.

Where we'd once danced so close to *"Caminito."*

So I was sitting there on the top rail thinking about nothing, but really thinking about nothing but Jack, as Midnight was frisking happily with two other young stallions behind me.

I was wearing my horse clothes (clean ones), boots, and a dark felt Stetson.

He rode up beside me.

I felt my heart respond.

Accelerate.

To be honest, I wanted to leap in front of him, right onto his saddle, and hold him close, but I didn't. I knew that his brother had been killed in Prescott, and I didn't know exactly what to do or what to say.

I smiled.

"I missed you," he said.

Well, that was that!

I jumped onto his saddle, as Night held steady, and I buried my face into Jack's chest, and I held him as close as possible.

I felt his hand gently in my hair.

Then I leaned back and looked into his eyes.

"I'm sixteen now, Jack."

Which I knew he knew.

"I know," he said.

Then he smiled his smile.

"That's the problem," he added.

Then he lifted me up, off the saddle, and lowered me down to my feet at Night's right flank.

"I need some time to figure myself out," he explained.

He was serious.

"I'll wait," I said.

Since I was just as serious.

He nodded, dismounted, tethered Night, and took my hand.

"Red Star's been shot," he warned me.

Then we walked back together to the big house.

[Moonlight]

Editor's Summary

Tuesday, July 28th

According to the Tucson *Daily Citizen* and every other newspaper in the territory, Philip Whitson was elected today as the territory's congressional delegate, receiving 78% of the vote to 18% for Jason Mitchell. Mr. Whitson was a last-minute fill-in candidate after the tragic death of Edward Shannon, the territorial Attorney General, who died preventing a brazen jailbreak attempted by the notorious gunman Damien Stark on July 17th in Prescott. Mr. Whitson was formerly Edward Shannon's legal consultant, and he ran for office on the same "statehood" platform as his deceased friend and employer. It's widely assumed that the electorate was greatly affected by Edward Shannon's death and that this sympathy contributed greatly to Mr. Whitson's resounding victory.

Chapter 41

Running Brook

Tuesday, July 28th

Jack came into Running Brook's little room at the back of the big house. It was late. It was the same night that Jack had returned from Prescott with Red Star and Jim.

I was sitting in the small room with my grandfather. We'd been discussing Red Star's improving condition. Running Brook had been tending to John's wound and prescribing traditional Tohono O'odham herbal potions.

Which were working.

Jack knocked on the open doorway, and I was surprised to see him. When my grandfather nodded, Jack entered. It seemed as though he was expecting him. Then my grandfather nodded a second time, and Jack sat down in an old wooden chair.

Where he waited.

Respectfully.

There was something on Jack's mind, which was obvious even to me.

Running Brook poured a small tumbler of port and took a long slow drink, enjoying every drop. Then he poured a small glass for each of his two guests, and we also drank the sweet dark wine.

Then my father's father looked at Jack as if to say, "Speak."

So he did.

"I need some time."

That's all he said, and I had no idea what he meant, but my grandfather did.

To give them some privacy, I rose to leave, but Jack shook his head "no," so I sat back down in my place.

He looked at Running Brook.

"I've seen a darkness within my own blood that I never knew existed. I feel uncertain about what to do with my life. About what to do with my abilities."

Jack, like Red Star, always seemed to be the kind of person who knew exactly what he wanted, and then immediately went about doing it. I was surprised by his uncertainty, by his admission of doubt, and by his willingness to share such things with me.

He looked directly at Running Brook.

"I've also scarred a young girl's life, and I'm fearful that I might do it again."

It was clear that he was referring to the girl back east.

As well as Moonlight.

Then Jack and I sat within the weak lamplight and shadows and waited.

Running Brook seemed to understand the problems, and he responded, as he often did, by telling a story.

Beginning with a question.

"Do you know *why* Grey Wolf sent John to live with the Apache?"

Jack seemed unsure of the connection to his own situation, but he responded exactly as I would have responded.

"To learn."

Running Brook nodded.

"Yes. When Grey Wolf was a young boy, he was captured by our enemies, and he lived with them for several years."

Jack was surprised.

So was I.

"When he returned to his family, he was a confused and uncertain young man. So he went off by himself and spent a year in the mountains."

Like me, Jack clearly got the message.

But Running Brook amplified anyway.

"Sometimes, Jack, prayer and time and reflection can direct one's heart and replenish one's soul."

Jack nodded gratefully, but he was still uncertain about something.

"But Red Star," he remembered, "came back from his time with the Apache *without* his father's confusions."

It was a question.

"Yes, Jack, because John was different from his father, just as you are from your brother."

Jack understood, then he thought about leaving Rising Sun.

"It'll be hard," he admitted, "to tell my friends."

He looked over at me, which I appreciated.

"They already know," the old man said.

So I thought about it, and I realized that I *had* sensed that something was bothering Jack ever since we got back, but I figured it was worry about Red Star's wound.

Or maybe that girl back east.

Jack looked back at Running Brook.

"Everything'll fall on you and John."

Meaning Rising Sun.

Meaning taking care of things.

My grandfather smiled.

A rarity.

"John'll be fine. Jack. He's done it before, and so have I. I'm not dead yet."

Jack smiled as well, as Running Brook continued.

"Besides, you were planning to go back to Rutgers anyway. Instead, you'll take some time to educate your heart and your soul."

Satisfied, Jack stood up and looked down at the old man.

"I'm grateful," he said simply.

Running Brook wasn't finished.

He was serious.

"Do you like to kill, Jack?"

"No."

"Then don't pretend that you might."

Jack nodded, then he left us in silence.

[Dark Sky]

Chapter 42

Red Star

Wednesday, July 29th

I felt better, but still weak, and Running Brook had insisted that I spend the afternoon resting in bed.

Which I did.

Eliza brought me lunch and changed my bandages.

Which was a great comfort.

She was sitting at my bedside when Jack came into my room.

I knew he'd been to see Running Brook the previous night, and I knew why he'd come to see me. To say goodbye. He was dressed in black and ready to ride.

He nodded politely to Eliza, then stood at the foot of my bed and wasted no time.

"I'm riding out."

"I know."

"Do you think it's best?"

"Yes. Solitude might remind you not to confuse your virtues with the failings of others."

He seemed pleased.

"Which way will you go?" I asked.

"South, then west. Into the desert, into the mountains.

Jack looked over at Eliza Mecham.

"Eliza has asked to stay at Rising Sun," he explained, "and I told her that she's welcome."

"Good."

Jack, of course, knew my heart.

He knew the love in my heart.

"Thank you both," she said softly.

Then Jack came over to the side of my bed and shook my hand.

It was always hard for us to part.

"Be careful," I said, "then come back."

"I'll do both."

Then I reminded him.

"It's bad luck to watch a best friend ride out."

He knew.

He walked to the door and turned.

"Till I come home again, John," he said.

"*Vaya con Dios.*"

Then my best friend left my bedroom, leaving me alone with Miss Eliza Meacham.

[John Red Star]

Chapter 43

Moonlight

Wednesday, July 29th

I knew he was leaving again, so terribly soon, and I was doing my best to be brave. To be stoic. Just like a brave Tohono O'odham girl should be.

But it was hard.

I was sitting on the front porch of the big house.

Waiting.

The new twilight had dimmed the valley, as if it was also dimming my world.

I heard him come up behind me. I knew he'd been off in John's bedroom saying goodbye.

Now it was my turn.

It was just an ordinary Wednesday in late July, but I was wearing my prettiest Papago dress. Traditional beige hide with fringe, with bright colored beads that my mother had sewn on this morning.

"You're a Tohono O'odham princess," she said, when I put on my headband and turned around.

"Yes," I thought to myself, "a princess whose love always seems to be riding away."

Jack came down the steps and looked at me directly.

"You're very beautiful, Moonlight."

Well, what do you say to *that*?

Maybe nothing.

Maybe "Thanks."

Maybe, "Then why are you leaving me again?"

But I said nothing, and he changed the subject.

"John's healing fast," he said, as if he didn't know what else to say.

"Yes, I believe he loves that Mormon girl."

"Yes, and she loves him."

"Yes."

He looked at me as if he had something important to say.

"I'm not sure what'll happen, Moonlight, but I have the feeling that there's something for us together. Eventually."

No one, of course, wants to hear the word "eventually."

When I said nothing, he continued to try and explain himself.

"For now, I need to get away for a while."

"How long?"

"Five months."

I took it stoically.

"If you could wait for me," he continued, "we can figure things out."

It seems to me that men are always trying to figure out things that don't need much figuring.

"I'll wait," I assured him, as I'd done yesterday at the stables.

"Is it fair?" he asked, as if he knew it wasn't.

Surely he was aware that there were other young men at Rising Sun who'd noticed that I'd become a young woman during the past year.

Who were interested.

"I'll wait," I repeated, "but there's one thing before you go."

He wondered what I meant.

"Kiss me goodbye."

"I've thought about it many times," he said.

"So have I.

He bent over and softly kissed my mouth, lovingly, as I lifted my hands to touch his face.

It crushed my heart with both happiness and desire.

Yes, it was something that I'd imagined many many times, but it was far better than my imaginings.

Then it was over.

Jack stood up, took Night's reins, and saddled up.

Once mounted, he looked down at me again.

"I'll be back at the beginning of next year," he promised. "January 1st."

I said nothing.

He looked at me intently. His black Portuguese/Irish eyes fixed into my dark Sonoran eyes, and he spoke for the final time before he left.

"I believe, Moonlight, that I love you more than anything else in this world."

Which was lovely to hear.

Thrilling.

Then he rode off into the twilight and left me sitting there in my pretty clothes on the front porch of the hacienda.

In my heart, I knew that he'd come back for me.

Why, I wondered, are men always so strange and difficult?

[Moonlight]

Chapter 44

Arizona Sundown

Wednesday, July 29th

I was out checking the herd.

Everything was fine.

Suárez had done a great job keeping things in order while I was gone, and I was very pleased.

Especially pleased because I knew that Jack and John would also be pleased.

I stopped and stared off at the far end of the valley, which was now streaked with amazing purples, reds, and oranges. It was another brilliant Arizona sunset. Red Star once told me that it's the clay in the desert soil that makes Sonoran sundowns so red.

I'd bet that he's right.

But what do I know about such things?

Then off in the far distance, I saw Jack riding the final crest into South Pass, where he stopped and looked back over the valley. I wondered if he could see me, so I waved my hat over my head, and Jack did the same. I knew he was leaving today, but I really didn't know why, and I really didn't know for how long.

Hopefully, he'll be back real soon.

Then I noticed another dark rider on the opposite ridge sitting on a rather restless black stallion. It was Moonlight on Midnight. She spotted Jack and waved her hand over her head, Jack did the same.

I had the feeling that he knew she'd be there watching him leave.

Then Jack turned away and headed into the pass.

But he hesitated.

As if reconsidering what he was doing.

Or did I imagine it?

Who knows?

Then Jack continued on his way, into the mountains, into the red Arizona Sundown.

[Jim Ellis]

Editor's Note

Jack never returned to Rutgers, but in the years that followed, Jack and I kept in touch at least twice a year. I wrote on Jack's birthday, and he wrote on mine. Sometimes we wrote at Christmas.

As for me, when I graduated from Rutgers College, I didn't follow the inevitable paths of so many of my classmates into the law, or the ministry, or various mercantile endeavors. Instead, as planned, I followed in my father's footsteps as a newspaperman. I'd never wanted to be anything else. I felt that the dissemination of the truth was a noble vocation. Initially, I served at the *Sun* as a do-anything-I-was-asked-to-do clerk, and eventually I assisted my father at the city desk. Then, when Bill Stockton finally retired, I took over his "West of the Mississippi" national news desk, even though I'd never been west of the Allegheny Mountains. But my school year with Jack had made me greatly interested in everything that was happening on the old frontier.

As for Jack, he came back from his sojourn into the mountains exactly when he said he would. January 1, 1886. Later that year, when

Moonlight turned seventeen, they became engaged. I was the one, of course, who had to tell Jennifer the news, and she took it hard. She considered writing to Jack, but eventually decided against it, and I did my best to be a comfort.

The following year, Jack and Moonlight were married at Rising Sun Chapel. Two years after that, Moonlight had their only child, a daughter named Maria in honor of Jack's mother. Later that same year, my cousin Jennifer married as well, marrying one of our old Rutgers friends, Lewis Carter, now a civil lawyer, who also knew Jack during Jack's only year in New Jersey.

Out west, Jack with his close friend John Red Star continued to run their various operations at Rising Sun, and, as far as I could tell, he was happy in his marriage and perfectly content with his rancher's life.

Sadly, I never saw him again.

Editor's Epilogue, 1912

In the end, Arizona got what it wanted, but it took much longer than its citizens would have wanted.

On January 6th of this year, 1912, New Mexico Territory was officially granted statehood. The following month, on February 14th, Valentine's Day, Arizona Territory was also officially granted statehood. Unfortunately, Jack Shannon didn't live to see it. He died two years ago at the age of thirty-five when he was out riding his herd during a thunderstorm and was struck by a fluke bolt of lightning. According to Jim Ellis, the ranch's cattle driver, Jack died instantly, falling from his horse.

Requiescat in pace.

When the tragic news reached the east coast, once again I was the one obliged to tell Jennifer the terrible news. She tried to be brave about it, but it wore on her hard. I did my best to help. Her husband Lewis had died the year before, after falling on the icy front steps of the Newark Courthouse. As far as I was aware, they'd had a contented marriage, both loyal and supportive of the other. Nevertheless, it was a marriage with something missing, something probably unspoken, specifically Jennifer's secret longings for someone two thousand miles away. It was also a childless marriage, as Jennifer had miscarried twice.

Now Jack was dead.

Four months later, Jennifer contracted pleurisy and began to fade herself. She never gave up, but the pleuritis was relentless. Jennifer Cameron, without a doubt, was the bravest, kindest, and most fun person that I'd ever met. As Jack once said, she was also "smart as a whip," and her musical talents were obvious to everyone and highly-regarded. Since I'd remained unmarried, I took an indefinite hiatus from the *Sun* to be at her side.

One afternoon, as she was lying on the living room couch in her parents' home, she took my hand.

She had a request.

A dying request.

"I want you to write the truth, Erick."

I didn't know what she meant.

"About Jack."

I still didn't know what she meant.

"About what happened the year he left us."

I thought I already knew what happened, and I wasn't exactly sure what she wanted from me, but I said "yes" anyway.

Of course, I said "yes."

She looked into my eyes.

"You'll have to go out there, Erick."

Fine.

She died three days later.

The last day of December.

So I did what she wanted, even though I wasn't exactly sure *what* I was doing. I extended my hiatus at the *Sun* and took the train west across the country into Arizona Territory.

It was January 1911.

The year before Arizona became the 48th state.

I'd been a newspaperman my entire adult life, and I knew how to track people down. From Prescott, I went down to Rising Sun, where I was welcomed by John Red Star, Moonlight, Dark Sky, Jim Ellis, and Padre Luis Delgado, who was close to death himself. Running Brook had died a few years earlier. At first, John Red Star, although perfectly congenial, was a bit wary about my purposes, but, in time, he seemed to feel that the truth should be told.

That Jack would want it that way.

Later, I went to Prescott and talked to Philip Whitson, now retired, who'd worked relentlessly for Arizona statehood and was much revered throughout the territory. I also tracked down Clifford Pierce and Douglass Tyler. Pierce, the one-time deputy in Gayleyville, was now a successful farmer on a small spread near San Simon. Tyler, who'd been the US Deputy Marshall in Elfrida on the day that Jack faced down Damien Stark, had retired to a quiet life on the edge of Tucson.

All were helpful.

All were, it seemed to me, honest, despite certain memory lapses. During my four-month stay at Rising Sun, I was made perfectly comfortable among those who did their best to remember 1885.

Moonlight: At the age of forty-two, Moonlight was now half-owner of
Rising Sun Ranch along with Red Star. She was also the ranch's

horse breeding expert. As one might have expected, she was both lovely and charming. As well as beautiful. It was easy to picture her and Jack together in my mind's eye. It seemed as natural as sunlight, as natural as moonlight.

Jim Ellis: The one-time Texan ran the ranch's herd of about eight hundred head. He was always affable, always ready to talk about Jack. Years ago, around the time of Jack's marriage, he'd married a Pima woman named White Dove, and they now had six children, most of whom worked at the ranch. On the day of Jim's wedding, Jack and John had given him a third interest in the herd, mostly long horns back then, as a marriage present. Jim told me that Jack had spent most of his adult life as a contented hard-working rancher, but that there'd been two subsequent "adventures" (as he put it) that he would only discuss if Red Star approved. Since they didn't relate to 1885, I never pressed my luck with Red Star. Maybe some other time.

Dark Sky: Jim's best friend, also married, had taken Coyote's place as the trainer of select young Tohono O'odham braves, still known as "warriors," who served as security for the Rising Sun Valley. Over the years, he'd also become Red Star's right-hand man, and he had nothing but fond memories of Jack.

Maria Shannon: I also met the elegant daughter of Jack and Moonlight, who was now married to one of Dark Sky's braves and had a daughter of her own, Jack's granddaughter, named Moondancer.

Coyote: I only met once with the aged Coyote, who was polite, yet mostly silent, unwilling to discuss anything about the past, "which is already written in the desert sky."

Red Star: Most importantly, of course, was John Red Star, the current patriarch of the valley, who'd married Eliza Mecham on the day she was properly baptized, two months after the wedding of Jack and Moonlight. He was initially, as already mentioned, the most reticent of my sources, but eventually, it was John Red Star who told me the truth, which was later corroborated by Philip Whitson, about what had really happened in Prescott, Arizona, on the night of July 17, 1885:

Chapter 45

Jailbreak

Friday, July 17th

It was the middle of the night.

Maybe three o'clock.

I watched a rough-looking man armed with a rifle walk up the deserted street in Prescott and enter into the Sheriff's Office, which also served as the city jail.

I didn't like the look of it.

Then three well-armed riders came down the same street, leading two saddled horses behind them, entering the dead-end alleyway beside the jailhouse.

A blind alleyway.

They went down to the end, turned around, and waited.

I waited as well.

It was hard to see clearly from my position. The moonlight was faint, but there were two outside lamps that managed to disperse some of the dark shadows in the passageway below.

Eventually, Edward Shannon, dressed in a suit, walked down the same street and turned into the same alleyway.

I was stunned.

Yet silent.

There was a handgun at his belt.

Edward walked down to the riders, nodded, and they did the same.

We all continued to wait.

A few minutes later, the same man who'd entered the front of the sheriff's office, a man named Hank Yolt, exited the side door of the jailhouse into the alleyway. He was immediately followed by Damien Stark, who was carrying a .45 in his good left hand.

Edward said something to Stark, which I couldn't quite make out. It seemed clear that Stark and Yolt were ready to mount the waiting two horses and ride away with the other three riders.

Then a dark figure appeared at the street end of the alleyway and stepped into the moonlit corridor.

Facing six men.

One of the riders lifted his shotgun.

"Hold it right there, mister," he called out.

But Jack continued walking.

Then he stopped.

"Stark!" he called out.

Stark turned and immediately recognized him.

"You!" he said.

He seemed delighted.

Jack said nothing.

I suppose by then, Jack had seen his brother and was trying to comprehend what was happening right in front of him.

Stark spoke again.

Clearly gloating.

"I told you I'd go free, you stupid bastard."

Jack paid no attention. He just stared at his brother for an explanation.

Edward looked at Stark.

"Quiet, you damned fool."

Stark wasn't happy about it, but he knew that Edward was still in charge, so he went silent.

At least, for the moment.

Edward turned back to Jack, attempting to explain himself.

"He did some work for me."

Then Edward noticed the rider with the shotgun was pointing it at his brother.

"Put that down!"

The man lowered the barrel.

Edward turned back to his younger brother, trying to be reasonable.

"Look, Jack, I can't allow myself to be implicated. You've got to trust me. You're my brother."

Which astonished Stark.

Who smiled.

"Brother!"

"Shut up!" Edward warned him again.

But Stark was fed up with Edward, and he ignored him.

"Well, Mr. Retribution," he taunted Jack, "who do you think paid me to drop Judge Dolan? And anyone else who got in the way, like that stupid marshal?"

Jack said nothing, but I knew him better than anyone.

He was stunned.

So was I.

Once again, Edward tried to wake up his brother to his own sense of reality, speaking with authority.

"Listen, Jack, there's a side of politics that you could never understand. Fools like you and Whitson think that elections are won by appealing to the public, but that's not how it works."

Stark was clearly enjoying Edward's unsuccessful attempts to win over his brother.

He spoke again.

Chillingly.

"Brackden was supposed to be next."

Meaning the Prescott sheriff that Edward had sent down to Phoenix on a fool's errand.

Once again, Jack was stunned into silence.

Edward made a final appeal.

"We're brothers, Jack, and I need your help now. I'm asking you to step aside. I'm not going to Yuma, Jack. I helped to build that hellhole."

Jack's response was short and simple.

"Never."

Edward's five men readied their weapons.

It was time for me to get involved.

I was watching guard that night from the roof of the mercantile store over the alleyway. I stood up in the darkness with my Winchester ready.

"No one move," I warned them.

I really didn't believe it would prevent what was coming, but I wanted them to know that Jack wasn't alone.

Everyone froze.

For the moment.

Finally, with the .45 in his left hand, Stark made a move on Jack. There was an instant and violent exchange. Everything happened in such a violent flurry within the darkened moonlit alleyway that it's not perfectly clear exactly what happened.

I believe it went something like this:

Even before Stark could fire his weapon, Jack drew his Peacemaker and shot him in the right wrist and left thigh, exactly as he'd done in Elfrida. Stark, in agony, dropped his weapon and fell to the ground. Then Jack also shot Yolt, who fell dead to the ground near Stark, who was now sitting in the dirt holding his reopened wounds.

At the same time that Stark had made his initial move, the rider with the shotgun went to fire at Jack, so I hit him flat in the chest and he fell from his horse to the dirt floor of the darkened alleyway. Then Jack shot the rider next to him, who also fell dead to the ground, and the third rider immediately lifted his rifle over his head in submission.

Yelling, "Enough!"

Somewhere in the midst of all of this, Edward had apparently shot me with his Smith & Wesson. I was struck hard in the left shoulder and the impact twisted me around and I fell back to the edge of the roof where I struck the back of my head. I was momentarily unconscious, partly hanging off the edge of the roof.

Edward, who must have been somehow impervious to everything that was happening around him, took aim at me once again, and Jack shot him.

Without hesitation.

In the forehead.

Which I could see from the roof as I revived myself.

Jack was horrified by what he'd done, and he stared down at his brother's dead body.

"I've killed him," he said softly.

In disbelief.

"He would have killed me, Jack," I called down from the rooftop.

Which he knew was true.

Which made him accept what he'd done.

Despite the pain in my shoulder, I managed to sit up on the roof.

"I'm coming down, Jack," I called down.

But Jack said nothing.

When I got down to the alleyway, Jack was still standing in the same place, still facing the harmless Stark, and his three dead accomplices, and the last remaining rider, who'd dropped his weapon to the ground.

Jack was still holding his Colt .45.

"Jack," I said.

He seemed to snap out of it and looked over at me.

"How bad is it?" he asked.

"I'll be all right, but you'll need to clear the alleyway with that idiot sitting on his Morgan. I'm afraid I won't be much help."

I looked over at the last rider.

"Get down and come over here."

He dismounted immediately, then he and Jack threw the other two dead riders over their saddles, while I stood watch over the now-silent Stark, who'd tied a bandana around his still bleeding thigh.

When the dead were secured, I looked at the third rider.

"I don't care who you are, just take these men out of town and do whatever you want with them."

He understood.

He mounted, and I looked at him cold.

"Never mention a word of this to anyone, or we'll come after you."

He nodded.

Then he led his train of five horses and two dead bodies down the alleyway to the main street, leaving behind the dead bodies of Hank Yolt and Edward Shannon.

When he was gone, Jack stepped over to Stark, kicked his Colt over to me, then kicked the man sharply in the thigh. The murderer cowered in pain.

Jack was Jack again.

He looked down at Stark.

"If you say a word about this, no one will believe you, and I'll shoot you dead in the courtroom. Then the town will give me a parade."

Stark was in no mood to argue.

Satisfied, I went into the sheriff's office and helped revive the deputy, a young man named Evan Conrad. I told him that I'd just witnessed an attempted jailbreak that had been prevented by Edward Shannon who'd been tragically shot by Damien Stark in the alleyway.

"Get Stark," I said, "and bring him back in here. Then take care of the body of Edward Shannon. Then forget that I was ever here."

He listened carefully, then nodded.

"Don't deviate," I warned him.

"I won't," he assured me.

So I left the office.

I walked back to the street-end of the alleyway, and Jack came down to meet me. Stark made no attempt to move. When Conrad came out the side door, he looked around and saw the dead bodies of Edward and Holt. Then he helped Stark back into the jailhouse.

Satisfied, Jack and I left to wake up the town doctor.

[John Red Star]

Chapter 46

Governor Tritle

Friday, July 17th

He thought it over.

We were standing in the governor's living room in the middle of the night.

Jack had just told us what had happened, and it would be hard to discern who was in more shock.

Me or Governor Tritle.

My closest friend was dead. In the process of attempting to free a notorious murderer from his jail cell. Shot by his own brother.

I sat in a chair attempting to fathom Edward's betrayal, attempting to fathom why I had never even suspected the corruption at the heart of the man that I'd worked with every single day for the past eight years.

The governor, still a bit groggy, wearing a robe over his sleeping clothes, seemed equally at a loss. Four years ago, he'd replaced John Fremont as the Territorial Governor, and he done his best to deal with all the problems in the territory. Especially what was known as "lawlessness." But recently, he'd been involved with the so-called "Thieving Thirteenth" territorial legislature, and even though I felt certain that he was free of all the corruption that had come to light, he'd still been damaged politically.

Guilt by association.

Now, like me, he'd lost a man he'd considered a friend.

He looked at Jack, as if uncertain what to say.

"How's your Papago friend?"

"He's with the doc. He'll get through it."

The governor nodded, clearly relieved, then he sat down on his couch and looked back at Jack who remained standing in the middle of the room.

Ever-stoic.

Within his own sense of shock.

"What made you suspicious?"

"We learned that my brother had sent Sheriff Brackden out of town on some bogus assignment down in Phoenix. So we started keeping watch at the jailhouse every night."

"Was Brackden involved?"

"I don't believe he's involved."

"I'm sorry that you've had to go through this, young man."

His sincerity was obvious, and Jack appreciated it.

"Don't lose sight," Tritle continued, "of all the good you've done. Keeping a violent man like Stark in jail will save lives and make Arizona a better place."

Jack didn't respond, but he had a question.

"Did either of you ever suspect my brother was up to something?"

"Of course not, Jack," I assured him.

Tritle was a bit more circumspect.

"There were rumors."

"Of what?"

"Of strong-arm stuff. Wielding political power. But never anything like this. Nothing like murder."

He seemed stunned by his own use of the word "murder."

Which seemed a seemingly impossible possibility.

But now it was a reality.

"Why did he want Judge Dolan killed?" Jack asked.

I let the governor explain.

"Dolan was a political rival, a man with a lot of influence."

"A man," I added, "who might have affected the upcoming election."

Jack understood.

I'm sure we were just confirming what he'd already assumed.

Silence took over the room.

Finally Tritle, a man of action, looked up at Jack.

"What would you like me to do?"

"I want you to announce that Edward died thwarting the jailbreak."

I was stunned once again.

I couldn't believe what I was hearing, and neither could the governor.

Jack continued.

"If the truth comes out, it'll wreck our hopes for statehood, which is what *everything* has been all about. Let the public think that Stark killed Edward. He'll deny it, of course, but it won't matter. Don't even charge him with the crime, just let his trial for the murders of Judge Dolan and Marshal Caldwell go on as planned next week. You've got plenty of witnesses to secure a conviction."

"What about you, Jack?" Tritle asked.

"Leave me out of it. Red Star too. We were never there."

"But Edward will seem like some kind of hero."

"Who cares? It's the future of the territory that matters."

Jack looked at me.

"Whitson, you'll need to take his place and win the election."

It seemed so preposterous that I didn't even respond.

Then Jack turned back to the governor.

"We can't have the US Congress thinking that we're all corrupt out here. That the Attorney General of the territory hired a gunman to murder a judge."

Tritle thought it over.

He looked back at Jack.

"Are you sure about this?"

"Yes, I want nothing to do with it."

Tritle acquiesced.

"Fine, then we'll do it."

He also added some advice.

"I know this is terribly difficult for you now, son, but God only holds us accountable for our own failings. Don't blame yourself for what your brother has done."

"I'll try not to."

The governor stood up, they shook hands, and Jack left.

It broke my broken and betrayed heart to ponder what the young man was going through, having learned the truth of his brother's evil heart, having been forced to kill him to protect his best friend.

So I sat there and said a prayer for all of us.

[Philip Whitson]

Appendix

Chronology:

(Compiled 11/10/1911, as best I'm able. – ER)

1796 – Matthias Padraig Shannon born in Missouri, Louisiana Territory

1798 – Grey Wolf born in a small Tohono O'odham village on the Sonoran Desert

1814 – Matthias Shannon joins the US Army Cavalry

1815 – The Battle of New Orleans (1/8)

1824 – Matthias Shannon leaves the army as a captain, encounters Grey Wolf in the Santa Rosa Mountains, they establish a "blood oath," then secure a Mexican land grant to Rising Sun Valley in the Sauceda Mountains

1825 – Grey Wolf builds the Rising Sun reservoir, farming begins

1826 – Matthias Shannon purchases a hundred head of cattle, ranching begins

1830 – The Rising Sun Chapel is built for Padre Luis Delgado

1846 – The Mexican War starts, Rising Sun remains neutral

1848 – The Mexican War ends, Arizona is now the western half of New Mexico Territory

1850 – Grey Wolf establishes a treaty with the Apache

1852 – Matthias Shannon marries Kathleen Handcock of St. Louis, Missouri

1853 – Edward Shannon is born at Rising Sun

1861 – The Civil War begins, Kathleen Shannon dies from a rattlesnake strike, Edward Shannon is sent to a boarding school in St. Louis

1863 – Arizona Territory is created

1864 – Matthias Shannon meets and marries Maria Barcelos of Rio de Janeiro; Grey Wolf marries Yellow Dawn, a young widow at Rising Sun

1865 – The Civil War ends (4/9), Jack Shannon is born (7/4), John Red Star is born (7/14)

1866 – Jennifer Cameron is born in New Brunswick, New Jersey

1870 – Moonlight is born at Rising Sun

1873 – Young Jack Shannon sees a man gunned down in Tucson, later that year his mother Maria Barcelos Shannon dies of consumption

1875 – Matthias Shannon, age seventy-nine, falls from his horse in the Saucedas and dies

1876 – Yuma Prison opens, Wild Bill Hickok is killed in Deadwood (8/2)

1877 – John Red Star, age twelve, spends a year with the Apache

1878 – John Wesley Hardin is sentenced to twenty-five years in Huntsville Prison; Grey Wolf, age eighty, and his wife Yellow

Dawn die of smallpox; Running Brook oversees Rising Sun in trust for Edward, Jack, and Red Star

1880 – Jack, age fifteen, goes to Tombstone to meet with Doc Holliday

1881 – Billy the Kid is killed (7/14), the Gunfight at the O.K. Corral takes place in Tombstone (10/26)

1882 – Jesse James is shot in the back of the head by Robert Ford (4/3), Jim Leavy is ambushed by John Murphy in Tucson (6/5), Johnny Ringo is found dead in the Chiricahua Mountains (7/13), Dallas Stoudenmire is killed by the Manning brothers in El Paso (9/18)

1883 – On John Red Star's eighteenth birthday (7/14), Jack and John are officially invested by Running Brook as the co-proprietors of Rising Sun Valley and Rising Sun Ranch; Edward Shannon, as requested, receives a significant financial compensation as his own inheritance

1884 – Jack Shannon confronts the Reicher Brothers in Gayleyville, Jack travels east to matriculate at Rutgers College

1885 – Grover Cleveland inaugurated (3/4), Edward Shannon is killed in Prescott (7/17), President Grant dies in New York State (7/23), Luis Rodriquez, Richard Brady, and Damien Stark are hung in Prescott

1886 – Jack Shannon returns to Rising Sun (1/1), engaged to Moonlight

1887 – Jack Shannon marries Moonlight at Rising Sun

1889 – Maria Shannon born to Moonlight and Jack Shannon at Rising Sun, Jennifer Cameron marries Lewis Carter in New Brunswick, New Jersey

1906 – Frederick Tritle, the former territorial governor, dies in Phoenix (11/18)

1910 – Jack Shannon, age thirty-five, is struck by lightning and dies instantly; Jennifer Carter dies of pleurisy in New Brunswick, New Jersey

1911 – Erick Ramsey, a national news editor at the *New York Sun*, travels to Arizona Territory to write the true story of Jack Shannon and 1885, he spends four months at Rising Sun and also visits Prescott, Tucson, and San Simon

1912 – Arizona statehood (2/14)

Publisher's Note, 1914

Publisher's Note to the Third Edition, 1914

Erick Stuart Ramsey

For the many who have asked for more information, the late Erick Ramsey was born in Manhattan, New York City, on August 29th, 1864. Like his father, he attended Rutgers College in New Brunswick, New Jersey, where he served as the editor of *The Targum*, the college newspaper. During his sophomore year, he was the roommate and close friend of John Shannon, a young rancher from Arizona Territory. After graduation, Ramsey followed in the footsteps of his father, Warren Ramsey, as a newspaperman. Eventually, he took over the city desk at the *New York Sun* from his father, before serving as the paper's national news editor for news "west of the Mississippi."

Locally, Ramsey covered many significant news events, including the Great Blizzard of 1888, corruption at Tammany Hall, the completion of Grant's Tomb, the deadly fire and sinking of the *General Slocum* in the East River, the construction of the New York City subway, and even the founding of the Bronx Zoo. Previous to the publication of his popular and best-selling *Arizona Sundown* (1912), Ramsey had published two other books: *Rutgers and the Founding of the Sport of Football* (1905) and *The Sinking of the General Slocum* (1907).

Much admired by friends and colleagues, Erick Ramsey never married, but remained especially devoted to his cousin Jennifer Cameron Carter of New Brunswick, New Jersey, to whom he dedicated *Arizona Sundown*. After her death four years ago, he confided to close associates that "I have no qualms admitting that if I hadn't been Jennifer's first cousin, I would have hoped to marry her someday. But, of course, the fates had decided otherwise."

Ramsey died earlier this year, February 14th, after having been tragically stuck by a runaway hansom in front of the main offices of the *New York Sun*. His publishers are hopeful that this brief appended *In Memoriam* for Erick Stuart Ramsey will also serve as an *In Memoriam* for all those most dear to him, as described in this book, notably his cousin Jennifer Cameron Carter and his dear friend John "Jack" Shannon.

Requiescat in pace.

About the author

William Baer, author of over forty books, has been the recipient of a Guggenheim Fellowship, a Fulbright (Portugal), a fellowship in fiction from the National Endowment for the Arts, the T.S. Eliot Award, and the Jack Nicholson Screenwriting Award. His various books include *Times Square and Other Stories*; *Advocatus Diaboli*; *Psalter: A Sequence of Catholic Sonnets*; *The Heretic*; *The Dark Knight of Assisi*; *The Gravedigger*; *Classic American Films*; *Luís de Camões: Selected Sonnets* (translations from the Portuguese); the Jack Colt mystery series (*New Jersey Noir*); and the Deirdre mystery series. He is a graduate of Rutgers, NYU, South Carolina, the Johns Hopkins Writing Seminars, and USC Cinema. He was also the founding editor of *The Formalist*, the director of the St. Robert Southwell Summer Workshops, and the film critic and poetry editor at *Crisis*.

His other writings have appeared in a wide range of literary, religious, and/or cultural journals including *The American Scholar, Chronicles, First Things, The Hudson Review, The Kenyon Review, London Magazine, Modern Age, National Review, The New Criterion, Ploughshares, Poetry, Quadrant, The Southern Review, The University Bookman, The Virginia Quarterly Review,* and *The Wanderer.*

He lives happily in a log cabin in northern New Jersey and loves pizza, books, sports, and chocolate.

Also by the author

Catholic-Themed Novels by William Baer:

Advocatus Diaboli

The Heretic

Jacinta

The Dark Knight of Assisi

Selected Other Novels:

New Jersey Noir

New Jersey Noir: Cape May

New Jersey Noir: Barnegat Light

The Gravedigger

Novel

Murder in Times Square

Murder in Nashville

Annie Oakley Mystery

Mary Pickford Mystery

Central Park

Companion

The Sweet Science

Equinox

WILLIAM BAER

Selected Other Books:
Times Square and Other Stories
One-And-Twenty Tales
Psalter: A Sequence of Catholic Sonnets
Formal Salutations: New & Selected Poems
Classic American Films: Conversations with the Screenwriters
Elia Kazan: Interviews
Luís de Camões: Selected Sonnets (translations)
Writing Metrical Poetry
Conversations with Derek Walcott